THE GOLD OF AKADA

THE GOLD OF AKADA

A JUNGLE ADVENTURE NOVEL: ANJANI, BOOK ONE

JOHN RUSSELL FEARN

THE BORGO PRESS

MMXII

THE GOLD OF AKADA

FIRST BORGO PRESS EDITION

Published by Wildside Press LLC

www.wildsidebooks.com

DEDICATION

To Peter Ogden

CONTENTS

CHAPTER ONE
THE WHITE GIANT

1932

The air was quivering with both the tropical heat of Central Africa and the reverberations of the drums. Drums, echoing through the primeval forest, their exact situation undetectable to the white man who sat flung in his rattan chair, his hand gripping the half-filled glass on the okume-wood table before him.

"Blasted natives," he whispered. "And out to get us, Ruth. They've been trying it ever since we struck this part of the jungle."

The young woman addressed did not answer. She was half afraid to. As the wife of Mark Hardnell, she was little better than a target for insults and abuse. She sat half-crouched on an upturned crate in a corner of the tent, her dark hair damply untidy on her forehead, her blue eyes darting about her in frightened wonder as the message of the distant drums continued.

Suddenly Mark swung on her, twisting round in his chair. He was a big, powerful man in the early thirties. Even in normal circumstances he was not a pleasant man, overridden as he was by ambition—and just at present he was unbearable.

"For God's sake, Ruth, stop those kids bleating!" he yelled at her. "We don't want to give away our position. And put out that damned lamp!"

Ruth began moving, extinguished the oil lamp, and then in the almost total blackness she stooped over the roughly crib in which two infants wailed lustily. They quieted a little under their mother's touch.

"You *would* have twins!" Mark's sour voice came out of the clinging, stifling murk. "It would have been bad enough to have one kid on a trip like this, but you had to have *two*! Damnit, you knew back in Zanzibar what was going to happen. Why couldn't you have stayed there until the thing was over?"

"My place is with you, Mark," Ruth said quietly.

"Don't hand me that! You hate the living sight of me!"

"I'm still your wife, Mark, and prepared to live up to it. If I hadn't come out on this ghastly trip, you'd never have ceased to curse me when you got back to civilization. Whatever I do is wrong: I've grown accustomed to it!"

"Oh, stop yelping!"

"I'm entitled to," Ruth continued, her voice low but quite steady. "We wouldn't be here at all, lost in the jungle, but for your crazy idea of trying to find a lost city. Ivory, jewels, gold—!" Ruth laughed half hysterically. "That was what you said—"

"I was right!" Mark blazed at her. "I've got the plan,

and I trust the man who gave it to me. There *is* a city in this region somewhere. The hard part is finding your way, and these damned Bushongo boys are no help, either. Wonder what the devil M'Tani is doing all this time?"

He blundered across the grey darkness to the tent flap and looked outside. There did not appear to be any sign of the carrier boys in the little clearing. There was only the deep tropical night and the eternal message of the drums. Mark swore, then regardless of giving away his position, he yelled harshly:

"M'Tani! *M'Tani!*"

Something the colour of polished coal tar glided out of the darkness. The only things visible about the head boy were the whites of his eyes and his gleaming teeth.

"Where have you been?" Mark demanded, using the mongrel language M'Tani understood. "Where are the rest of the boys?"

"Gone, bwana. Umango tribe close."

"Gone, eh?" Mark spat. "Ratted on us, you mean?"

M'Tani did not understand. He was glancing fearfully around him. Only his loyalty to the white boss made him stay at all.

"I told you to discover what chance we had of escape," Mark reminded him. "Have you done that?"

"Yes, bwana. No chance. Umango much nearer."

"No chance?" Mark's eyes narrowed as he looked into the dark. "You mean this tribe is closing in, in a circle?"

The Bushongo nodded urgently, and seemed to

be making up his mind whether or not to run for it. Abruptly he reached a decision, swung around, and then fled across the clearing like a shadow.

"Come back here, you scum!" Mark roared after him, then as the noise of drums suddenly stopped, he too became quiet, gazing fearfully around him. The silence seemed awe-inspiring after the reverberation that had been so ceaseless.

Slowly Mark turned back into the tent. He collided with Ruth in the darkness.

"Get the kids," he said briefly. "We're getting out."

"But—where to? Where do we go?" There was utter hopelessness in Ruth's voice.

"I don't know. The Umango are all around us, closing in. We might escape. Be better out in the open fighting it out than hemmed in this clearing. You take the kids, and I'll carry what I can."

Mark picked up his .303 Enfield and strapped on cartridge bandoliers. Ruth did not go immediately to the twin sons, now silent in the corner; she moved instead to the bottled water, bully beef tins, and other provisions. In the darkness she began sorting them out.

"Why should the Umango particularly wish to attack us?" she asked after a moment. "We're doing them no harm."

"We're in their territory and not welcome," Mark's clipped voice retorted. "Our boys have all gone and left us to it. If we're caught, I don't know what will happen. Maybe a sacrifice, maybe anything. Come on, Ruth, how in hell much longer?"

"Ready, ready," she said quickly, putting two water bottles in the big haversack along with the provisions.

Mark lifted the tent flap, peering cautiously into the utter and eerie silence. Untrained in jungle lore, he did not hear the stealthy advance of hundreds of fantastically painted warriors. His first awareness of anything was when a barbed shaft, soaked in venom, crashed into his chest.

He gulped, uttered a strangling cry, then pitched over on his face. Ruth looked up in alarm from the rough crib from which she had been about to gather the infants.

"Mark!" she whispered; then in a sudden frenzy as she dashed to the tent opening: "Mark! *Mark*—!"

She stopped, seeing him lying face down in the rank grass. In the deep gloom she could detect that he was not moving.

"Mark—" She caught at his shoulders desperately and dragged on them—then another sound made her look up. The clearing seemed to be alive with shadows, sweeping in towards her.

Fantastic figures poured out of the dark. Powerful hands seized her hair, her shoulders, her arms, her legs. She screamed frantically, again and again, until the forest seemed to be echoing to her cries.

* * * * * * *

1952

Caleb Moon sat and sweated. There was not much else he could do in this stinking, tobacco-smoked café on the waterfront of Makondo in Somaliland. As he sat he drank and sweated some more. He was a heavily built man, inclined to corpulence, and dressed in a faded khaki-drill suit. A sun-helmet was pushed up on his damp black hair, His face was podgy, greasy, and unprepossessing. Dark eyes, black as sloes, darted about in eternally restless movement as though he were afraid of seeing somebody he did not like. In a sense this was true. As a trader of dubious scruples, dealing in ivory, diamonds, skins, or anything else that had a value, he had many enemies.

For nearly half an hour he remained slouched, hardly moving, watching either the men and women around him, or else the bead curtains that screened the outer door of the café. Then, suddenly, he straightened and got to his feet. A man and a woman, obviously Europeans, had just appeared and were looking about them. They looked surprisingly clean and cool in this oppressive den of seamen, half-breeds, and drifting women.

Moon went over to the man and woman and raised his sun-helmet briefly.

"Mr. and Mrs. Perrivale?" he enquired, with an unctuous smile. "Caleb Moon...."

"How are you, Mr. Moon?" Harry Perrivale's greeting was completely matter-of-fact as he shook the trader's damp hand.

"How do you do?" Rita Perrivale acknowledged, contented with a mere nod.

"Over here—" Moon motioned. "I have a quiet table."

He led the way to where he had been seated and dragged up chairs. There were one or two curious glances towards the well-dressed Europeans, then interest in them expired. It was too hot to be interested in anybody.

"Drink?" Moon asked, mopping his neck.

"Whiskey," Harvey Perrivale answered, and Rita named a soft drink. The waiter obliged, and then Moon sat back and breathed heavily.

"I was beginning to fear you weren't coming," he commented. "And that would have been a pity—for both of us."

"We were delayed." Perrivale sipped his drink. He was a man of thirty-five, sharp-featured, dark, handsome after a fashion, but spoilt by a dissolute mouth and poor chin. "From Port Durnford to here is quite a distance. Anyway, let's hear more of this proposition of yours."

"It is unchanged from when I explained it to you in Port Durnford," Moon shrugged. "I have a map showing a route through Central Africa to a lost city by the name of Akada. In that city there is gold and ivory for the picking up—but I am not a man of money. To fit out a safari to cross Central Africa takes a good deal of finance. You have backed tropical expeditions before now; I thought you might wish to back this one."

"Mmmm. I gathered that was it. What is there in it for me?"

"Fifty-fifty on whatever Akada contains. Surely that's fair enough? I have the map; you have the money. Neither of us can do without the other. Share profits."

There was silence for a moment. Rita Perrivale's grey eyes travelled over the assembled men and women at the tables and her sensitive nostrils twitched in disgust. She was a girl of infinite refinement, ten years younger than her husband, and not all sure what had been the matter with her when she had fallen for him. He was a millionaire, certainly, but that was not everything.

"Let me see the map," Perrivale ordered at length, but Moon shook his head and grinned.

"Wouldn't be good business, sir. You might have a photographic mind."

"What the hell do you mean?"

"I mean—bluntly—that I won't show it you unless we have an agreement. Your finance—my map."

Rita sat back and smiled rather bitterly. She was accustomed to these wrangles with traders and shysters on this torrid coast. Her husband, bored with millions, found he got a kick out of trying to add to them— hence he was known as the moneybags behind most of the expeditions into the interior. Usually he cleaned up something out of his risk.

"I don't see why you hesitate," Moon said, spreading his hands. "I know you've financed half a dozen expeditions into the interior—sometimes for zoological purposes, and once even for the Botanical Institute.

That's why I contacted you in Port Durnford when this map came into my hands. I'd have laid my scheme before you there, only—well, this is my territory. I don't belong on the high-class outskirts of Durnford where you and the lady live."

"I wish to heaven we didn't." Rita commented, sighing, and she looked away to avoid her husband's coldly reproving glance. Moon's gaze strayed to her. He liked her youthful figure in the white costume and blouse. He liked her aloof expression, blonde hair, and independent chin. He rarely saw a white woman in the course of his erratic career, and when one as good as this turned up—

"At least tell me where you got the map," Perrivale suggested. "I'm not financing anything so big as a safari right across the interior without knowing all the details."

Moon considered this, fingering his underlip gently, his sloe-black eyes on Rita. Then as she caught him out in gazing he said slowly:

"How I got the map is my business, Mr. Perrivale. All I will tell you is that I got it from a Bushongo who had been in a recent safari. He found it amidst a lot of other things in a wallet lying in the clean-picked bones of a skeleton. According to the other things in the wallet, the map was made twenty years ago. In that wallet, what bit could be read of various things like insurance certificates, letters, airport passes, and so on, everything was dated 1932. So, time passes on."

"And this Bushongo came straight to you?"

"All those who matter do so." Moon aimed a level glance. "I'm a trader, Mr. Perrivale. It pays me to keep in with the black boys. I get lots of tips that way."

"And how do you know this map of yours is genuine?"

"Because Mark Hardnell was not the kind of man to go into the bush without good reason. He was looking for Akada, maybe for the same reason that *I* am now hoping to look for it."

"Hardnell?" Perrivale scratched his receding chin. "Mmmm—yes, heard of him, though I was I was only a boy at that time. He was a rather crazy, drunken roamer well known in Zanzibar, wasn't he? Had a wife, I think, who went everywhere with him."

"Dunno," Moon said. "But I *do* know any map found on him must have a genuine purpose. He seemed to have got partly on the way to his objective, too, judging from where that Bushongo found the skeleton. Don't know what happened. Savage tribe, maybe."

Silence again, Perrivale weighing matters up. Moon poured out some more whiskey and swallowed it quickly. Rita regarded him with that distant look in her grey eyes.

"Right across the interior, eh?" Perrivale mused.

"That's it. Across Kenya Colony into the Uganda Country, then into the Belgium Congo region. After that—" Moon checked himself with a grin. "Nearly forgot," he apologised. "That information has to be paid for, of course."

"There are more ways of getting a map, Moon, than paying for it," Perrivale reminded him, with an unpleasant smile.

The sloe-black eyes pinned him. Moon's voice was dead level: "Don't get any notions like that, Mr. Perrivale. I know men—and women too—get wiped out like flies around here for various reasons, and there's rarely an explanation, but that's because they're careless. I'm *not* careless. I know how to look after myself."

Perrivale nodded. "I can believe it," he said dryly. "And this safari you're talking about won't be any ordinary little thing, not to cover *that* distance. It's over fifteen hundred miles to the Belgian Congo from here."

"I know," Moon responded calmly. "That's why I can't afford it. It's also a good distance to where Akada stands—but surely it's worth it?" He leaned on the table, intent and earnest. "In Akada, according to what I know from the map and other details, there must be ivory and gold worth several millions sterling, if it can only be moved. That's the point. Moving it even when we get there. I can't afford that kind of help. You can."

"It'll need a partially mechanised safari," Perrivale said, and Moon nodded.

"It will, until we get so deep in the forest we can't use such things. After that we'll want the biggest army of tough natives we can find to do the carrying—Damnit man, it's surely worth fifty-fifty?"

"It's worth it—if I come with you."

Moon rubbed his mouth and mused; then Perrivale added: "I want to be sure after financing such an expedition that I get a good return. Your reputation, Moon, isn't exactly highlighted for honesty!"

"Nope—I wrangle where I can," Moon grinned. "But in this case I've no objection if you want to come."

His eyes strayed to Rita again. "Better bring your wife, too," he added. "Unless you trust leaving her behind."

"Meaning what?" Perrivale demanded, his eyes sharp.

"Meaning a pretty woman with her kind of shape is in danger from every damned louse once her husband isn't around."

"The men aren't like that in our section of Port Durnford!"

"They're like that anywhere, Mr. Perrivale. There's more scum in Durnford than you'd think—and as you'd find out if you left your wife behind." Moon shrugged. "Just a suggestion. I'm looking out for your interests."

"Kind of you," Perrivale sneered. "She comes anyway. She always does wherever I go. I agree with you that a pretty woman isn't safe alone."

Moon grinned comfortably, and thought of the thousand miles of journey ahead when necessity would throw him in constant contact with Rita Perrivale. It would make the journey really pleasurable.

"It's settled then," Perrivale said, getting to his feet. "I'll make arrangements for the safari. It will start only when you produce your map. Agreed?"

"Agreed," Moon responded, rising. "I'll be around this dump for some days yet, waiting for news from you. I'm ready whenever you are."

Perrivale shook hands and then jerked his head in a completely unmannerly fashion to Rita. She withdrew her hand from Moon's and felt she wanted to smear her palm down the side of her white skirt. She had a sense of feeling defiled.

Moon watched the two disappear beyond the bead curtains, then he sat down again and dragged out a cheroot, He lighted it, grinned to himself, then ordered more whiskey.

"Such a lot of things can happen in the interior," he told the native waiter, thinking out loud.

"Yes, bwana," the waiter agreed and wondered vaguely what the hell the trader was talking about.

* * * * * * *

A safari, sadly depleted from its original strength, made its way slowly along the jungle trail, through the midst of the ugly baobab trees, past mushrooms as large as umbrellas, close by flowers issuing an intoxicating perfume and as viciously active as a steel lash if one came too near, And in all directions were the screams of parrots, the chattering of monkeys, the distant roaring of a challenged lion, and the eternal tsetse-flies hovering in clouds, particularly in the cooler spots and above the eedoo glades.

It was the African afternoon—blazing hot, relentless—even though the sun itself was masked by the dense foliage and the twisted, cable-like lianas overhead. The safari moved slowly, gleaming Bushongos at its head, their dark skins rippling with perfect muscles as they wielded their machetes.

The Europeans at the rear of the long trail moved with lassitude. So far they had escaped the ever-pestilential malaria: drugs had seen to that, as far as Harry Perrivale and Rita were concerned. Caleb Moon seemed to remain on his feet because of the amount of whiskey he consumed. He just sweated everything out of his system and kept on going—but the spirits had done many things to his temper since the long gone day when the journey into the interior had started.

In fact, his temper was the cause of the woefully thinned safari, and when the safari halted its journey for the night, Perrivale said so in no uncertain language. Caleb Moon listened to him, seated on the camp-stool in his own camp, and going through the routine of looking for chiggers' eggs in his faded drill suit. The eggs, hatching at body heat, could drive a man or woman to frenzy if not 'deloused.'

"Less drinking would help, Moon," Perrivale said, and his dissolute mouth tightened.

Moon grinned. "What d'you expect a man to do in this blasted frying pan? Run around with his tongue out waiting for Mr. Perrivale to say, 'You can have your water ration now'? I drink when I like, Perrivale—and that'll be often. You've no authority over me. In fact, without me you won't get anywhere! So get back to your tent and shut up!"

"This safari is mine," Perrivale retorted. "Thanks to your damned temper, it's cut in half. The boys are scared of you, flaring up at the least thing. They're flesh and blood the same as us—and we can't do without them. We'll need every man we can get when we reach Akada."

Moon dragged on his examined shirt. "I've handled this kind of scum all my life, Perrivale, and you only get results by making 'em afraid of you. I know my business."

"Lessen this safari any further and we may as well go right back home," Perrivale snapped. "Watch yourself, Moon, that's all."

Perrivale left, his mood black, and crossed the fire-lighted clearing to his own tent. Within it Rita was doing what she could with her damp tresses, She eyed her husband as he came in.

"Well, did you warn him?" she asked.

"Yes."

"I doubt it. You're as scared of him as these poor black devils outside. And a scared man in the jungle is no use to anybody."

Perrivale glared at her. She studied his reflection through the folding mirror in the lamplight.

"No use denying it, Harry," she added. "You've got plenty of money but precious little nerve. You've only come on this expedition because you think there is safety in numbers. Well maybe there was—until the safari thinned out so much. We can't have more than twenty boys left. If they go—"

"They mustn't," Perrivale interrupted, alarm in his voice. "If we were just left to find our way back—we—

we just *couldn't.*"

Rita finished playing with her hair and turned to him. There was contempt in her grey eyes.

"I wish I'd known you were so yellow when I married you," she sighed. "Unfortunately, the only yellow I saw was the gold you own. Moon, for all his faults, *is* tough."

"Good God, from the way you say that, one would think you prefer him to me!"

Rita shook her head. "I think he's a beast," she said deliberately. "And a drunken one too, but I do wonder if that isn't preferable to being cowardly. That's the one thing about you, Harry, I just *can't* tolerate!"

Perrivale said nothing. He knew she was right, but to a great extent his wealthy parents had been to blame. Whilst they had lived, they had brought him up in cotton wool, under the belief money could buy manhood for him. It had not—and this was the first time he had ever ventured into the merciless jungle. It had frayed his nerves, shortened his temper—

A scream from outside the tent suddenly made Rita start. Perrivale looked up in surprise. Getting to her feet, Rita hurried over to the tent flap and dragged it aside. At that moment she heard the thick, liquor-cracked voice of Caleb Moon shouting:

"You damned louse! I'll teach you to let the fire go down—!"

There followed the crack of a rhino-lash and a desperate scream.

"Bwana, I slept—I—" But the lash cut off the rest

of the words.

"Blasted scum!" Moon screamed, obviously inflamed with liquor. "The more that fire goes down, the more we stand to get attacked by jungle beasts! Sleeping? I'll show you—"

Again and again the lash came down, and in the light of the subdued fire Rita could see a black figure squirming under the onslaught of Moon's flashing arm. She also saw other black figures darting off like shadows into the jungle, scared of the white boss's fury. Rita looked after them helplessly, unable to call since she did not know the mongrel tongue they used.

"Mr. Moon!" she cried angrily, striding towards him. "Stop it! Do you *hear* me? Stop it!"

In his frenzy Moon took no notice. Rita strode on towards him and finally grasped his arm. He paused for a split second, and then swept his arm back and round, flinging Rita from her feet and sending her stumbling into the undergrowth. Dazed, she lay there, her shoulder throbbing from the blow.

The interval had been enough for the hapless black to make an effort to escape, but the vicious whip brought him down on his knees again. He chattered desperately for mercy, and did not get it. His chattering broke in screams again as the lash flayed across his naked back.

"Next time you'll keep a fire *going*!" Moon roared at him.

From his own tent Perrivale stood watching, then he suddenly yanked out the .38 at his hip and took aim.

At exactly the same moment Moon caught sight of him in the firelight. Drunk though he was, he was not so confused that he could not act fast. He dropped his whip and aimed his own revolver instead. Flame bit across the dimness, and with a cry Perrivale dropped his weapon and fell, clasping his leg tightly. He remained as he had fallen, his features contorted.

"Harry!" Rita cried in anguish, leaping up from where she had fallen. "Oh, Harry—"

Moon blocked her path, his thick arm encircling her shoulders from the front.

"No you don't!" he breathed, clutching her. "If that scared louse of a husband of yours has a parked bullet in him, it's no more than he deserves. I've been waiting for this—a legitimate reason for shooting him. You and me will keep going—"

"Let me go!" Rita kicked at him savagely, and the sharp points of her half-boots made him wince—but he did not release her. She struggled vainly to tear free, but only succeeded in being dragged all the closer to the trader.

Then something else happened. Moon saw it first and blinked. A second later he felt it. Something that seemed to be too hard for flesh and bone crashed straight into his face and sent him flying backwards. Half stunned, he flattened in the loam, sparks bursting through his brain.

It took him a second or two to recover. He twisted round and stared on something he could not believe. There was a newcomer in the clearing, white-skinned in the dim firelight, his only attire a leopard-pelt about his loins.

"What the hell?" Moon whispered to himself, sobering—then he staggered up and came floundering across the clearing. The newcomer, behind whom Rita was crouching, waited—but he did not strike out.

He was tall beyond the average, possibly six feet four, with power-packed shoulders and chest. His hair, roughly cut, was flung back from his broad forehead, secured with a thong, and was the colour of honey. The hilt of a crude-looking knife projected from the leopard-pelt.

Still Moon stared, unable to credit his senses. Rita backed away and hurried over to her groaning husband. Moon made a half move to follow her but the white giant moved also with one foot, barring the way. Moon peered at him, studying the well-cut features—then as fast as thought his hand blurred down to his gun, and he yanked it out.

Before he could fire the stranger's right hand shot out and closed round his wrist. The trader gasped as steel fingers tightened relentlessly and all but broke the bone. Then, heavy man though he was, he was lifted in the air and flung with savage force. He struck the bole of a baobab tree on the edge of the clearing, and dropped with half the senses knocked out of him. His gun had gone—so he did the only thing he could. He crept into the jungle and kept on going, completely unable to understand what had happened.

The white stranger turned at last to where Rita was

making ineffectual efforts to drag her husband into the tent. With perfect ease the giant lifted the wounded Perrivale in his mighty arms and bore him to the camp bed, laying him down. Rita was too intent on trying to ease her husband's pain to pay any attention to the white man who now stood with folded arms, watching impassively.

"He—he got me—in the leg," Perrivale panted, his face sweating. "I don't know if the bullet's still there. Take a look."

He relaxed again on the bed, setting his teeth. Rita looked at him helplessly, her knowledge of first-aid and anatomy practically negligible. Then she seemed to become aware of the silent white man watching her. His advent should have startled her, and indeed it had at the time, but just at the moment her whole attention was given over to her husband.

"Can't you do something?" she entreated. "He's been hit in the leg. Look at it."

The finger pointing towards Perrivale's blood-soaked trouser leg was enough to get the white giant on the move. He went down on his knees beside the camp bed and tore Perrivale's trouser leg up the side, then he examined the leg itself, wiping away the blood with a piece of trouser leg. The injury looked worse than it was really, but even so Perrivale had suffered a wound that had gouged deep into the calf and only just missed the bone. The bullet itself had apparently passed on.

Rita, seeing the extent of the damage, turned aside,

and heated water on the oil cooker. Then she bathed the wound and bound it up with wadding from the medical kit. Perrivale gave a taut little nod of thanks, the pain of the injury still pretty considerable.

"Thanks, Rita," he said—and, glancing up at the white giant, "and thanks to you, too. Just who are you, anyway? You're white."

Rita eyed the giant with his rippling muscles, keen blue eyes, and finely cut chin. He had blond hair tied back with a thong.

"He's wonderfully developed," Rita murmured, admiringly.

The giant made no comment and turned to go, but Rita caught his arm.

"Please—don't go yet! We want to learn more about you. And besides, Moon might return. If he does, I don't want to be left to tackle him by myself, as I should be with my husband like this. It will be quite a while before he can be up and about."

The giant listened in puzzled interest, obviously trying to understand. Rita sighed, but she kept her small hand on his mighty forearm.

"Rita," she said, pointing to herself, then nodding to the watching man on the camp bed she added, "Harry. Now what is your name?" and, her eyebrows lifting inquiringly, she tapped the giant's broad chest.

"Rita—Harry," he repeated in a grave, deep voice that had none of the guttural intonation of a native. And, seeming to grasp the point, he added, "Anjani," and indicated himself.

"Anjani?" Rita looked interested.

"It means 'White God' in some native tongues," Harry said from the bed. "Don't let the fellow go, Rita—there's something queer about him being here in the jungle."

Rita increased her grip on Anjani's arm and tugged a little. Finally he seemed to understand, and, smiling, moved back into the tent and waited for what might happen next.

"We must teach him English," Harry said, relaxing again. "He certainly doesn't belong in this hell-hole, and I think we ought to find out why. But don't let him go, Rita—he's too useful."

Rita said nothing. It was just beginning to occur to her that, now her husband was wounded, a new cowardice would be added, strengthening the old, and weakening the man. With Anjani at his right hand, there was nothing to stop him keeping in the background whilst the mysterious white giant faced all the dangers.

CHAPTER TWO
ENTER TOCOTO

Caleb Moon had moved perhaps half a mile through the jungle, alert for any danger that might spring out of the night, when sounds ahead made him halt. He was no longer drunk—the things that had happened to him had sobered him—and besides he needed all his wits about him if he were ever to survive the countless dangers of the forest. He had no gun; his only weapon was his short-butted rhino-whip tucked in his belt, and, if he could get close enough to an adversary, there was also his hunting knife.

The sounds ahead made him draw his knife and wait, hidden by the dense bushes. The sounds came nearer, then Moon sucked in a breath of relief as he beheld not an animal but half a dozen black figures, hardly distinguishable from the night. They were evidently the Bushongo boys who had fled at his exhibition of temper.

"Stop—all of you!" Moon commanded, in their mongrel tongue, and rose up. He put his knife away and drew out his whip instead. The crack of the lash stopped the natives immediately.

"Now listen to me," he continued. "You are coming with me, as planned. Understand? We are leaving the white man and woman and continuing the journey to Akada with this small party. The white man is no longer of any use to me—he got the safari across the worst country. I can do the rest myself. And if any of you desert, those remaining will be punished. Understand?"

"We understand, bwana," one of the men answered.

"About time," Moon growled, knowing full well that the natives were loyal enough to each other not to leave punishment to innocent members. "That being so, we can keep on going. We have no food or provisions. I had to leave in a hurry. But there's plenty to keep us alive in the jungle until we strike a native village and can get some replenishment. All right, start moving, and remember what I told you."

"But, bwana, we move all day," the same native protested. "We sleep. Men tired and—"

"Don't argue with me!" Moon screamed at him. "I need sleep too, but I can't afford it. Move, I said!"

So the six Bushongos did as they were told, and certainly not with good grace. Moon felt a little safer with six brawny natives around him. It immediately lessened the ever-present danger from wild beasts or savage tribes.

And as he pushed on, Moon did a lot of thinking. As he had told the natives, the worst part of the country had already been covered and, according to the map, Akada lay about two hundred miles to the north. If he could only reach it, he remained convinced that he could get the necessary native labour to transport whatever ivory or gold there might be. The sight of the stuff would be sufficient guarantee to the natives that they would get a reward for their labours. But the matter of provisions had to be solved, and the natives, too, needed rearming with spears. The only hope in this direction was contact with a friendly native village up-trail. Moon, in fact, regretted only one thing—leaving Rita Perrivale behind. He had plans for her.

He frowned as his thoughts turned back to the white giant who had mysteriously appeared. To Moon the mystery was made doubly baffling, because he usually heard of anything unusual in the jungle, though not perhaps at this depth. On this trip he had penetrated further into the trackless waste than ever before.

Two hours later, as a fresh stream was reached, Moon called a halt. He was satisfied by this time that the natives would not desert again. The strategy of making those who stayed responsible for those who did not had worked. The natives were wary of him, but the knowledge of the treasures of Akada was a strong motivating force. Though the natives had no ideas of civilised values, they did know that ivory and gold meant plenty of prosperity for their particular tribe.

Just to make sure, Moon roped his wrist to that of the headman whilst they slept. Long trained to wake on an instant, Moon knew that any movement on the rope would arouse him. The headman knew it too, and made no effort to get away. In turns the remaining natives kept guard, but the night passed without any dangerous interruptions.

A breakfast was made of edible plants and roots, and the stream slaked rising thirst. To Moon, accustomed to whiskey, the water tasted filthy, but he had to drink it just the same. The only thirst-quencher on the next march would have to be the juice of fruits—so in the increasing heat of the torrid day the march resumed, Moon using his wrist-compass to check his direction and occasionally halting to study the map.

It was mid-morning when there came an interruption. Without warning a full-blooded lion leapt suddenly into the trail. Snarling, its mane bristling, it faced the startled Bushongo boys. They turned, blundering back over each other, none of them armed. By their very speed they escaped the lion's first lunge at them, which left Moon facing the beast. He tugged out his whip with one hand and his knife in the other, determined to sell his life as dearly as possible. He knew he could not escape backwards in time.

The lion crouched, measuring distance—but before he could spring something plummeted down from the dense foliage overhead and dropped cleanly astride the tawny back. Moon, prepared for a death battle, could only stand motionless and stare, bewildered by the vision of the same man he had seen the previous night, now wrestling with the giant snarling beast.

It was obviously not the first time the white man had been locked in mortal combat with the king of beasts. He anticipated every move and was ready for it, the muscles rolling on his mighty back, tendons taut on his great thighs and calves. First he was above the lion, then below it, but always keeping the bared fangs away from his body with one powerful, up-thrust arm. With his free hand he drove in a knife, again and again, into the lion's breast.

The frightful paws lashed and batted with force enough to knock the man over, but he dodged each blow and held on like a steel vice—until at last the stabbing blade struck home true to its mark, and with a final gasping roar the beast relaxed and became still.

Slowly the man stood up, wiping the knife blade on his loincloth. Then he turned and looked at Moon.

Moon stared back, the natives slowly coming to his side, and the longer he looked the more the trader became aware of differences in this individual. For one thing he had a clearly visible scar down the outside of his left arm, evidently a relic of some battle or other—a scar that the man of the previous night had certainly not possessed. Moon was sure of it. Though he had only seen the other by the firelight, he had seen his arms clearly and there had been no mark like this. Then there was the different loincloth—native-weave and not a leopard pelt.

"You speak English?" Moon asked finally, and the giant shook his head as he came forward. In features he was identical to the man Moon had previously seen, except that they seemed to be cast in a somewhat fiercer mould. His hair, too, was blond, and kept from falling over his face by a thong.

English having failed, Moon tried various local dialects, and finally the mongrel tongue of the Bushongo. Here he got a result. The giant understood it, though not very clearly.

"Tocoto," he said, indicating himself. "I—I follow you. Through treetops."

"So I gathered," Moon answered. "Why?"

"Akada. You go to Akada. I have been near you often and heard you speak of Akada. I know that you go there now."

"What's that got to do with it?" Moon snapped.

"Tocoto want to reach Akada. Tocoto has always wanted to reach Akada, but did not know way. You do. Tocoto come along with you."

"Let me get this straight," Moon said slowly, realising that he must handle this giant carefully. "You've been following us. Why? Because you know we have a map?"

"Because of safari. Then I heard you talking; decided to stay close. I come with you, Tocoto wants to reach Akada."

"For what reason?"

"Jewel," Tocoto replied ambiguously. "The jewel of Akada can give Tocoto power over all the tribes of the jungle."

"Tribal superstition, eh?" Moon looked sardonic.

"Many men seek jewel of Akada. None find. None know where Akada is—but you do. I go with you."

"You realise you are a white man like me?" Moon asked. "Where do you come from?"

"Tocoto lord of the Banwui tribe. Soon, when Tocoto has jewel of Akada, he will be lord of the whole jungle. The jewel has great power. M'Untino, the witchdoctor, has himself said it."

The explanation did not satisfy Moon. The presence of the white man—in fact, two white men—of such superb physique in the heart of the African jungle had definitely fired his imagination. The jewel of Akada itself he did not even think of twice: most of the tribes were always looking for something that would give them domination over their enemies.

"You—you live with the Banwui tribe?" Moon questioned.

"Tocoto always lives with them. Tocoto their lord."

"But you're *white*! You can't belong to *them*! You have the features of a European—even an Englishman."

"Tocoto a Banwui," the giant answered simply. "We go now—to Akada. I could take map and go alone, but I do not know how to use object on your wrist, nor do I know what signs on map mean. I trust you. If you betray Tocoto, Tocoto will kill you."

There could not have been anything plainer than this. Moon was saddled with the mysterious white giant whether he liked it or not, and apparently Tocoto knew only the primitive law of kill or be killed.

"You have always lived with the Banwui tribe?" Moon insisted.

"As long as memory go back," Tocoto answered. "Tocoto bring much power to his tribe when he has the jewel of Akada."

Moon still remained where he was, ignoring the white giant's move towards the jungle. Finally Tocoto came back to him, impatience of his handsome, bronzed face.

"You delay," he said harshly. "Why?"

"I am lost," Moon answered, with a sly smile. "Only one can show me the way—a white woman a day's march to the rear."

"White woman?" Tocoto repeated, surprised. "There are other whites in the jungle?"

"There are, including one exactly like you who, when I last saw him, was holding the white woman prisoner."

Tocoto hesitated, still surprised. "White man like Tocoto? No white man is like Tocoto. He is lord."

Moon frowned. It was perfectly obvious that this man and the one of the previous night were identical twins, but their existence here in the heart of the jungle remained, of course, a complete mystery to the trader. The fact that neither brother had ever encountered the other seemed incredible, and yet—and yet that seemed to be the case. It was possible that the density of the jungle had made it that their paths had never crossed, and that natives seeing one, or the other, had always taken it to be the same man and therefore thought nothing of it.

"I repeat," Moon said after a while, "that I cannot go on without white woman. Fetch her to me and we go to Akada. No other way. If the white giant like you is there, destroy him. He is evil, trying to cheat you of power."

"Tocoto wish to meet this white giant," Tocoto muttered, bunching his great fists. "None can challenge Tocoto. The white woman is a day's march?"

"Day's march south," Moon assented. "She alone must be brought. Any other whites must be destroyed. You go, and I will wait."

"Yes, you wait," Tocoto agreed. "If you go without Tocoto, he find you later and kill you—" And with that the young giant swung up into the dense foliage and vanished from sight. There was a rustling, a rising chattering of monkeys and the twittering of birds, then the forest was comparatively quiet again.

"Bwana stay here?" asked the nearest Bushongo, and Moon gave a nod.

"We camp until white man return with white woman. Lay in what fruits you can find, especially those with juice. We all need a drink."

The natives started moving to obey his orders. He himself, though tormented by the desire for whiskey, was none the less in good humour. Since Tocoto had dropped out of a clear sky, he might as well be used. With his simple, childish mind he would probably do as ordered on every occasion—and in trying to fulfil his present instructions he might bring Rita Perrivale back with him. The only thing against it was that by this time she might have been torn to pieces by jungle beasts, or the other white giant might have claimed her for himself.

"Can but see," Moon mused, half aloud. If she *is*

alive, and is brought back here...." He grinned to himself at the thought.

* * * * * * *

Tocoto himself, using all his jungle instincts, kept due south by the only means he knew—following the sun. No ordinary man could ever have singled out a camp under such vague directions, but Tocoto was not an ordinary man. He had the forest instinct of the tribe with whom he had been brought up.

So, by means of diverse clues—pausing only for sleep when night came—Tocoto came ever nearer to the camp of which the trader had spoken. Altogether it took him three days and nights, crossing and re-crossing, before he finally arrived at the clearing where there stood two canvas tents and, outside them, all the paraphernalia of a camp. Silent, crouched in the trees, Tocoto's blue eyes searched the space below.

There did not appear to be anybody in sight, but his sharp ears soon picked up the murmuring of voices. He hurtled to a tree directly over the two tents and froze rigid, listening. The words did not make sense to him, spoken first in a high voice, and then in a deep one.

"This is grass.... This is a bed."

"This is grass," repeated the voice. "This is bed."

Tocoto scowled, not understanding. Finally he dropped down lithely from the tree branches and crept silently towards the tent from which the voices were emanating. The trees prevented him casting any shadow on the canvas, so he searched around until finally he discovered a small gap where the tent lacing had fallen apart. Carefully he peered through the narrow crack, and then started in amazement.

Within the tent a woman in shorts and a sleeveless silk blouse was seated in a canvas chair, and before her, satisfied with kneeling, was a white man of immense stature and yellow hair. A little distance behind them a man lay stretched on a bed, a white man, dishevelled, tired-looking, listening to what the woman and man had to say.

"We are in the African jungle," Rita said deliberately.

"We are—" the giant hesitated and laughed a little. "We are in—African jungle."

"You speak English well," Rita said in delight. "Which seems to prove it may be your original tongue. Now, we'll try again. Slow but sure, eh?"

Tocoto's eyes narrowed. So the fat trader had not been lying. Here was the second white lord, identical to himself. To Tocoto it was a mystery and a decidedly unpleasant shock. Knowing nothing of the biological side of life, the notion of twins was completely lost to him. He only saw another man who might very soon challenge his territory.

Tocoto retired silently and leapt into the protection of the foliage, then he sat thinking. When Moon had summed Tocoto up as a fool with the mind of a child, he had made the greatest mistake of his life. Tocoto had high intelligence, far above that of the natives with whom he had been brought up, and though he had conformed to jungle standards, he had all the natural powers of reason—and the cunning of a jungle animal. So, as he listened to the voices from below he worked out a scheme, and finally it brought a hard grin to his face.

The easiest way to deal with woman would be to let her think he, Tocoto, was the man to whom she was now talking. That would simplify the journey back to the trader and would not mean her constantly trying to escape. As for the white giant himself— Well, Tocoto had an entire tribe at his bidding, and they could surely deal with one white man. Swiftly, silently, so the white woman would not know there had been an exchange? Yes, that was it! As for the other white man, weedy and ill, he could soon be accounted for.

His mind made up, Tocoto straightened, leapt for the nearest branch and thereafter began to hurtle through the treetops with dizzying speed in the direction of his own tribe's village. He gained it six hours later, as the shadows were lengthening and the savage heat of the day was commencing to abate. Dropping lightly to the ground, he sped across the open spaces where the women of the tribe were still at work with their naked children around them, and finished his run at the giant elk horn hung by strips of dried skin to a crude wooden bracket. Blowing through it with all his lung power, he sent a wavering note over the village and across the nearby jungle, and in response the men and women of the Banwui came hurrying out to see the reason for the summons.

Tocoto, lord of them all, waited until they were assembled, and then he spoke, keeping a wary eye on M'Untino, the only man in the tribe who ever dared to question his orders. In fact, M'Untino was hardly worthy of the name of man, He was wizened, unguessably old, dried up with sunlight, and as evil as the incantations he all too frequently invoked.

"I want twenty of the strongest warriors," Tocoto announced, speaking freely in the tribal language. "To the south is a white man, so like me I might have gazed upon myself in a lake of clear water. He will challenge my power, your power. The only way this challenge can be met is for him to be brought here and sacrificed to Mantamiza...."

Tocoto turned and bowed in reverence to the hideous wooden effigy not two hundred yards away. Immediately the tribe bowed also and murmured:

"Mantamiza! Mantamiza!"

"I shall take the place of this interloper," Tocoto continued. "And what is more, I shall soon bring to you that thing of great wonder—the stone of power over every tribe of the forest—the jewel of Akada!"

"Akada! Akada!"

"I have a white man who knows where Akada lies," Tocoto continued, "but before he can guide me there, he must have a certain white woman. She is protected by this man who looks like me. Now you know why he must be brought here and why I must take his place.... There is also another white man. The great Mantamiza would not welcome him as a sacrifice, so he can be killed. One swift blow of the spear!"

"How long with Tocoto the Mighty be gone on his journey to Akada?" croaked the witchdoctor.

"Many moons, father. But I shall return with the jewel of Akada."

"While you are gone, young one, I shall control," M'Untino decided. "Give me that power."

"It is given," Tocoto replied, raising his hand; then he turned back swiftly to the assembled warriors who had come forward from the ranks. "Arm yourselves!" he ordered. "We will strike by night when the white ones are unprepared. Mantamiza has commanded it that way."

Mantamiza was a word that always worked magic for Tocoto—he had discovered that long ago. For himself he was inclined privately to treat the horrible effigy with scorn, but he dared not to do so publicly. He might—in fact, would—incur the wrath of the witch-doctor, and once that happened life for Tocoto would not last very long.

Whilst the men prepared he rested, refreshing himself with meal bread and fermented fruit juice; then at sunset he set forth at the head of his chosen score of black warriors. This time he kept to the jungle trail. The swift arrival of night prevented any recourse to treetops where everything depended on clear vision ahead.

Tocoto permitted no halts, since the work had to be done by night. He himself was not fatigued, and since the natives had done nothing but laze for the past few weeks, a hard march would not do them any harm.

Meantime, entirely unaware of what was heading towards them, Rita, her husband, and Anjani were sleeping. Anjani, introduced recently to a bed for the first time in his life, found it a more comfortable spot than a tree-fork, and the net was useful too for keeping away the flies. He lay stretched upon it in the tent formerly used by Moon, his great body relaxed, his slumber profound. It was an unnatural sleep for him; away from his treetop, his senses seemed somehow dulled.

In her own tent Rita was half awake, afraid to doze in case her husband needed something. He lay in the bed near her, breathing deeply. Apparently he was gradually recovering, but had some distance still to go. So it was Rita who caught the first sounds coming from the jungle—different sounds to those of the denizens of the night. The stealthy cracking of branches, the brushing of bodies against massive leaves. Normally Anjani would have been instantly awake, but tonight he had relaxed too well.

Rita sat up and listened, her heart thudding. The air crawled with heat even at this early hour of the morning. Its stifling enervation carried the sounds clearly. She glanced towards the dim outline of her husband, her eyes accustomed to the dark, He was sound asleep, his hand closed around the .38 that he kept constantly by him for protection in his present helpless condition.

Rita glided across to the rifle by the wall, ready and oiled for instant use. She slipped the cartridge bandolier over one shoulder and, rifle in hand, padded in her bare feet to the tent opening and looked outside. The sounds had ceased now, and nothing was visible. Anjani's tent lay silent and ghostly in the dimness. She hesitated whether or not to call. If some savage tribe were in the nearby jungle, it might precipitate things. So she waited—

Then she swung with a gasping scream at a sound behind her. It was the tearing of canvas as a knife flashed down the further end of a tent. Her scream stopped halfway as she saw the white skin of Anjani, and, faintly, his silhouette.

Without saying a word he grasped her in his powerful arms, swept her off her feet, and bore her out of the tent. The rifle dropped from her grasp and the bandolier slipped from her shoulder.

"Anjani, what are you doing?" she demanded, thumping his great chest and feeling certain he would grasp some of the meaning of her words. "Anjani! Put me down!"

He did, at the clearing's edge, but only for a moment. He stooped so that his shoulder caught her about the middle, then he straightened. Dangling helplessly down his back, the back of her legs held by one of his hands, she found herself borne into the silent forest. Yet she still did not cry for help, convinced as she was that Anjani had some good reason for his strange behaviour.

Meanwhile, Anjani himself had just awakened to the awareness of hands to his throat and vitals—and instantly he was alert with all the alertness of a jungle beast faced with death. For one split second his night-accustomed eyes took in the view of half a dozen natives around him, then with a mighty heave he tore himself from the clutching hands and lashed out with his fists. He thought grimly that he would never forget again to sleep as did the beasts of the jungle!

His first blow smashed the jaw of the nearest native and sent him sprawling over the bed where it collapsed with the impact. Stooping, Anjani thrust his head between the knees of the next nearest man, and then straightened up, flinging the man helplessly through the air, where he crashed into his confusedly moving comrades. After that they became the target for blows that landed with smashing impact. They descended across their faces, on the base of their skulls, in their unprotected stomachs.

Then Anjani leaped back. Having gained room to turn round he whipped out his knife and drove it deep into the breast of the native who came hurtling after him. As the man fell the blade came free and landed in the throat of a second warrior.

But they kept on piling relentlessly into the tent, forcing Anjani further and further back, until at last his knife was taken from him, and again he had only his sledgehammer fists and mighty muscles to rely upon.

Desperately though he fought, and though the tent came down in smothering folds in the midst of his struggles, sheer weight of numbers and the iron strength of his adversaries finally overwhelmed him.

He found his wrists fastened behind his back with viciously thin thongs. Then his ankles were similarly tethered. Finally he was hauled to his feet in the gloom, breathing hard. He glanced towards the nearby tent that was curiously silent, then around him on the gathered warriors that had survived his retaliation.

"Who are you?" he demanded, and had to use a variety of tongues before he struck one which was vaguely intelligible to the warriors.

"Banwui," answered the spokesman. "You tagati—Mantamiza destroy. You sacrifice."

Anjani was silent, wondering why he was "tagati"—or bewitched. Not knowing anything about his twin, he just could not fathom the business at all—but he did remember Rita and called her name as loudly as possible.

Nothing happened. Her tent remained dark. The leader of the warriors looked in that direction and then jerked his head. Immediately Anjani found himself lifted on the shoulders of eight of the men, four a side, and he was borne into the forest, a heavy and constantly squirming burden.

Meanwhile, back in the silent tent, Harry Perrivale was lying shaking in mortal fright. Not two inches from his chest there stood a massive spear that had transfixed the bed and indeed would have impaled him too had he not made a subconscious twist to one side. The native who had done the job, convinced in the dim light he had succeeded, had then raced across to help his fellow tribesmen in dealing with the white interloper.

Now Harry Perrivale lay sweating and shaking. Always a coward even in the best of circumstances, his weakness at the moment made him doubly so. He licked his lips, nerveless fingers on a .38 he had not the strength to fire. He listened to the sounds in the jungle slowly receding.... Then the silence was back—sticky, cloying, relentless.

It took him several minutes to piece together what had happened, and even then it didn't make sense. He had seen the dim figure of the white giant, whom he had assumed to be Anjani, bearing Rita away—then had followed the attack by the single native, who had driven the spear at him. There could only be one answer, as far as Harry Perrivale could fathom it. Anjani had not been friendly really, in spite of seeming so. He had turned savage in the finish and swept Rita away, assisted by members of a jungle tribe.

Harry moved and sat up again. In spite of everything he still loved Rita, and though the jungle and physical violence frightened him beyond measure, he knew he could not abandon Rita to her fate any more than he could lie here alone and hope for a miracle.

So, shakily, he began moving. His trembling now was not so much from reactionary fear as genuine weakness, but he knew he had to master it if he were ever to try and save Rita or keep himself alive.

He began to gather provisions together, made sure his rather ineffectual .38 was fully loaded and that he had enough bullets to keep it supplied, then he limped out slowly into the darkness of the clearing.

CHAPTER THREE
THE PYTHON

Tocoto moved swiftly, Rita still over his broad shoulder. By this time she had given up trying to make him explain, however haltingly, and hung passively wondering where the journey was going to end. Then, presently, Tocoto eased her down and set her on her feet.

"Anjani, where are we *going*?" she insisted. "What about my husband? We've left him there alone."

Tocoto did not answer. He turned to continue the journey, but she caught at his arm. Then, for the first time in the confusion, she noticed something. In fact, she had seen it before when hanging over the giant's shoulder, but it had not then immediately impressed her; now it did so completely. The giant's loincloth was *different*. Rita stared at the native weave cloth in the dim light and her heart began to beat faster. There was also something peculiar about the arm she was still holding. After a moment she realised the tip of her thumb was in the midst of a deeply furrowed scar.

"You're—you're *not* Anjani!" she cried in sudden horror. "Like him, yes, but you're not him—!"

She turned to run back blindly into the jungle, but in two strides Tocoto had caught up with her and seized her shoulder savagely. She was flung against him and, thereafter, he never once released his grip. Protesting helplessly, she was forced on through the jungle, carried over the difficult regions, but never once released; and throughout the time the white giant who was identical to Anjani never uttered a word. So finally Rita gave up taking, and tried to fathom the mystery instead.

She failed—but things began to make a little more sense when at last, as the dawn was approaching, she found herself forced into a natural clearing wherein, protected from sudden animal attack by thorn bomas, there lay several natives and a white man. In the centre of the clearing a fire was flickering brightly, fed by a single native who had remained awake especially for this task. Caleb Moon stirred at the noise of their arrival.

"Tocoto bring white woman," Tocoto said in the native tongue.

The trader sat up, then got to his feet. He grinned widely and rubbed his podgy hands.

"Good work, Tocoto," he said. "I never thought you'd do it! What about the man who looks like you, and the other white?"

"Man who look like Tocoto with Tocoto's tribe. Make sacrifice to Mantamiza. Other white man dead beneath warrior's spear."

Rita jerked her head from one to the other, quite unable to follow the tongue, then her frightened eyes looked at Moon. He stared back at her lasciviously. She was dirt-streaked from the rough journey, and her bare feet were bleeding. What remained of her blouse and shorts barely served to conceal her.

"What—what do you want with me?" she asked huskily, as Tocoto released her. "What's all this about? Who is this man?"

"What do I want with you?" the trader repeated, and he smiled cynically. "My dear, what does a man usually want with a woman? As for this man, I think we might call him a rather stupid and gigantic baby. He doesn't understand English, so we can talk freely. His resemblance to the other man is quite remarkable, is it not?"

"They're twins," Rita said, trying to keep the situation in focus. "They must be!"

"So I think. However, since the twin has been taken by Tocoto's tribe as a sacrifice and your weak-kneed husband is dead, there's nothing you can do but come along with me, is there?"

"To—to where?"

"Akada, naturally. This is the whole purpose of this jungle trek. Out friend here believes only you know the way to Akada, which is why he has brought you here. That was a subterfuge on my part, I'm afraid. You see, Mrs. Perrivale, the journey can be so much pleasanter with a white woman as charming as yourself to accompany us."

Rita didn't answer. She remained looking at Moon fixedly as the daylight suddenly came into being. She could now see the hard grin on his face, and the animal look in his sloe-black eyes.

"Tocoto will come with us, of course," the trader added. "He has his own ideas about Akada. Later I will try and deal with him."

"You waste time," Tocoto said, breaking in on the conversation. "We go to Akada."

"When the white woman has rested," Moon answered. "I cannot force her, Tocoto. She knows the way, and if she will not reveal it, I am powerless."

"Tocoto make her speak—" The white giant made an arrogant stride towards her, but Moon checked him. Rita backed away, her bosom rising and falling stormily, her grey eyes bright with fear.

"You cannot travel far in that attire—or lack of it," Moon said. "There are plenty of tough vegetation leaves about. With thongs you can fashion something for yourself."

Rita was silent, one hand drawing the shreds of her silk blouse together. Her blonde hair had fallen in tumbled cascades about her tired, frightened face.

"And hurry it up," Moon added briefly. "We have to start moving again quickly, or else Tocoto will get annoyed—and he is not the type of man with whom I wish to argue. I could kill him, of course, since I have a knife and whip, but I think he might kill me first if I wasn't quick enough, and that would be most unpleasant. When you are ready, we will have breakfast, such as it is."

Rita knew she was cornered. Biting her lip in indecision she turned to the foliage and selected several of the giant leaves and tough vines with which to fashion garments and protection for her thorn-stabbed feet. Tocoto watched her impassively, and so did Moon— not so impassively.

"When we reach a native village which is friendly, you can have better clothing," he said, then he turned aside and with a crack of his whip set the natives on the move to gather together a breakfast of edible fruits.

* * * * * * *

Tightly bound about wrists and ankles, just as he had been when taken from the Perrivale camp, Anjani lay in silence in a filthy native hut. He could feel insects crawling over his naked body. Through the narrow opening of the hut, made entirely of grasses and sun-baked clay, he could see a gigantic fire being kindled in the centre of the village. Its ever-increasing flames shone luridly on the other huts comprising the village and the high walls of the stockade. As yet it was still dark, but the natives were busy. It was not often Mantamiza had so delectable a sacrifice. Fortune would indeed smile on the Banwui tribe once this night was over.

Anjani breathed hard, then he threw all his strength into his mighty arm muscles in an effort to snap the cutting thongs about his wrists. He was unsuccessful. Cramped, breathing hard, he relaxed again.

It seemed to him that nearly an hour passed, then there came definite signs of activity outside; the fire, now kindled to its greatest size, cast a livid, dancing blaze, Behind it, weirdly painted in the light, reared the hideous pagan god of Mantamiza. Gradually, then increasing in rhythm, there came the sound of tom-toms. Fantastically painted natives, armed with spears and shields, began the sacrificial dance round the fire, their chanting voices keeping time with the drums. Anjani recognised all the signs of a *m'deup* dance that would end in an insane orgy and a sacrifice. For a long time yet the ceremony would continue, growing greater in frenzy, watched over by the sinister M'Untino, the witchdoctor.

Knowing that he would be the guest of honour at the end of the dance, Anjani began to move again. He wished that he had his knife, but that had been taken from him long ago. He squirmed and twisted, his eyes moving to the flame-painted grass roof of the filthy dwelling; then, as the light grew brighter, he saw something not far from him: an ancient spear, corroded with age, which had no doubt belonged to the native who had once occupied this hut.

Immediately Anjani rolled towards it, and for the next ten minutes lay crouched in front of it, working his thongs up and down the battered metal spearhead. Finally, under the constant friction and the strain of his muscles, the thong snapped and his wrists were free. To undo his ankles was a moment's work, then he stood up and stretched his cramped limbs. Cautiously he padded to the opening of the hut and looked into the compound. The *m'deup* dance was still continuing, but on the fringe of the dancers there stood other warriors, isolated from each other, waiting for their turn to join in the gradually increasing frenzy.

Anjani gave a grim smile as he singled out a solitary native in the middle distance. He had a knife in his loincloth, which was the one thing Anjani needed. To reach him without attracting attention from the others should not be difficult. So Anjani began to move silently, keeping well in the dimness of the palisade until he was directly in line with the warrior. Since his back was turned, the native had no chance to realise what had happened when a massive forearm suddenly locked under his chin and a hand clamped relentlessly over his mouth. Struggling helplessly, he was twisted over and flattened on the ground, steel fingers now digging into his throat. He gulped and writhed and threshed, but all to no purpose with the grinning white giant on top of him. At last the writhing body was still.

Anjani took the knife, thrust it into his loincloth, and then vanished in the jungle, leaving the dancers in the midst of their wild lunging to the din of the tom-toms.

The distant rhythm of these same tom-toms was reaching Harry Perrivale, too, as he limped on his game leg through the night-ridden jungle. He realised now what a fool he had been to try to find Rita in the darkness. He had imagined that the way she had taken with the white giant must be clearly defined. Indeed, it probably was, but he had not the night-eyes necessary to detect it. And by this time he had hopelessly lost himself. He paused, listening to the distant drums, and wondering if they were meant for him or someone else. The only consolation was that they did not seem to be coming any nearer.

Another sound distracted him abruptly, a noise in the jungle itself and quite apart from the drums. He waited, his .38 ready, thanking heaven that his bandaged leg was far stronger than he had imagined. He desperately hoped the noise was made by some small animal. A second or so later he knew differently as something thudded from the trees only a few yards behind him. He twirled, gun ready. What dim light there was filtering from a foliage-hidden moon revealed a heavy, darkly-spotted animal measuring him carefully. It was a leopard.

Harry fired in blind panic, never bothering to take aim—then he started running desperately. The leopard, quite unhurt, bounded after him. Harry stopped again, flashed a glance over his shoulder, and then leapt side-ways into a thicket. In the darkness the leopard missing him for a moment—but only for a moment, then it caught the scent and came plunging through the dense undergrowth. Harry fired again without accomplishing anything, and went on running, tearing vines out of his way, dragging his feet from imprisoning creepers. Lithely, the leopard kept in pursuit, its temper rising as its prey kept escaping.

As he blundered on, trusting to the dense vegeta-tion to slow up the animal's movements, Harry got the impression that another leopard was following in the treetops. He could hear the rustle of branches overhead and the snapping of twigs. Then, with a sudden snarl of triumph, the leopard leaped out of the darkness and was upon him, bearing him to the rank undergrowth.

Harry struggled fiercely, his hands pushing help-lessly against the glossy, spotted coat. He knew he had not the strength to save himself. Then, miraculously as it seemed, the heavy weight was dragged from him. In the gloom he could see the dim outline of a massive white figure, pulling on the giant cat's tail with all his strength. Infuriated and hurt, the leopard twirled round and sprang forward, only to find the white tormentor was not there. The leopard hit the ground again with a heavy thud—then the white man made it his turn to leap, clean astride the animal's back. A knife gleamed momentarily in the dim light, moving up and down as the leopard screamed. Its savage struggling grew weaker, and at last stopped altogether. Slowly the white giant stood up and put his knife back in his thong-belt.

"Anjani—" Harry came creeping forward, a dishev-elled shaking figure. "Thank God! That brute would have got me if you hadn't arrived...."

"You should not have run away," Anjani answered, feeling for words. "Leopard not normally savage to—to man."

"Savage enough for me, anyway," Harry growled. "And how the devil did you manage to find me?"

"I hear gun," Anjani answered. "Came quick. I escape from Banwui tribe."

Harry rubbed his head in bewilderment. "There's something I don't understand, Anjani. Who attacked me back at the camp? Why did you take Rita away?"

There was silence for a moment, then came Anjani's deep voice in wonder.

"*I* take Rita? No."

"But you *did*! I saw you! You snatched her out of the tent just as I woke up. Then a blasted native tried to drive a spear through me!"

Since it was plain Anjani did not understand, Harry went into a full explanation, framing his sentences differently on several occasions so as to make his meaning perfectly clear. In the subdued moonlight Anjani's face was grim when the story was finished.

"White man like me here," he said, waving his arm in a wide sweep to indicate the jungle. "I must find. White woman in danger. Come. We find."

Anjani swung actively, but Harry caught his arm.

"I can't do it, Anjani. I'm still a mighty sick man, and I can't move much further."

"We move," Anjani insisted. "I take you—" and before he had realised it Harry found himself hauled over the giant's shoulder. Then Anjani began moving, travelling swiftly through the moonlight, pausing at intervals and listening, moving on again. It seemed to Harry that this kind of progress lasted for an hour and more before Anjani suddenly began climbing a tree.

In the uncertain silver light of the moon he began to swing from branch to branch, apparent not incommoded by the weight of the man over his shoulder.

"Where are we going?" Harry questioned after a while, closing his eyes as dizzying leaps across space were made.

"Me—I know. Follow in treetops."

So Harry said no more. He could not make head or tail of the crazy patchwork of foliage and vegetation below, most of it foundering in the deep shadows, but evidently the jungle-man who bore him could for he continued progressing without pause. After a while he spoke again.

"You and Rita—you go to—Akada?" he asked.

"We were, until Caleb Moon walked out with the map. Right now I don't know *what* we're doing. My only anxiety is to find my wife and clear up the mystery of this other man who looks exactly like you."

"I know Akada," Anjani said.

"You—you do? Then why on earth didn't you say so sooner?"

"I wait until you better. I saw Akada once—me a boy—I can find.... Lost city. Much gold."

"I know; that's the reason for going there—and evidently that's what Moon hopes to do as well. Why he's had Rita abducted, I don't know—or maybe I do. That dirty beast has been making passes at her ever since we left Makondo."

"We find," Anjani assured him. "Then we—"

The rest of his words were cut short as, in the dim light he missed his grip on the branch to which he had leapt. Instantly he hurtled down into the undergrowth, dropping heavily and flinging Harry from him. For a moment both men remained as they had dropped, dazed with the impact. Then Anjani began to rise, but he could not move forward. Something clinging was gripping him about the knees and he nearly overbalanced.

Harry saw what had happened at the same moment and gave a shout of warning. A giant python was squirming its way about Anjani's now struggling body, a python as thick as a palm tree and especially infuriated by the man who had accidentally dropped upon it from above.

Instantly Anjani knew his danger and tried to whip out his knife, but the strong coils wrapped relentlessly round his thighs and stomach prevented the action. Already he could feel the reptile's coils tightening inexorably and his breathing came only with tremendous effort.

"Gun— Gun!" he panted, straining with his mighty muscles to break free. "Kill! Kill!"

Harry nodded anxiously in the moonlight, holding the gun and looking for an opening. He did not dare shoot in case he hit Anjani instead. Meanwhile, Anjani himself was hampered by being only able to get at the reptile's head. Otherwise he would have coiled it about itself, even strangled it by its own constricting coils— but this was not possible, All he could do was hold the head and struggle to tear the jaws apart.

It was the moment when reptile and superhuman white man were equally matched—the snake with its terrible constrictive power and the man with his iron muscles. Harder he forced the jaws apart, and harder still, he tensed the muscles on his shoulders and arms. He knew that if he did not win this round, he was finished, for his strength was fast giving out, the terrific pressure about his middle preventing him drawing breath.

The coils edged higher, and tightened a little more. Anjani gulped, and his muscular power weakened ever so slightly. But he still held that head away from him. Once he released it the jaws would clamp about his neck with the relentless power of a steel vice and that would be the finish. Once give the python momentary freedom, and it would contract its muscles to the limit, squashing the prey in its coils to a pulp. But as long as the head was held, the snake was limited in its crushing tactics.

Anjani tried again with his flagging strength, ripping the jaws wider and wider. His main object was to smash the upper jaw if he could, and make it impossible for the monster to bite. The lower jaw, capable of infinite extension on elastic-like ligaments—for the purpose of consuming a prey many times its own size—could never be broken.

"Fire!" Anjani whispered, perspiration streaming down his face. "Fire—to head. Kill—"

He could feel himself going, losing the unequal struggle. His hip bones felt on the verge of cracking as the python constricted its coils. From chest to feet Anjani looked as though he were standing in the midst of rubber tyres marked in a black and gold pattern. Only his powerful arms were free, and they were no longer stretched in front of him, tensed and taut. They were giving at the elbow as the dreadful head swung in even nearer.

Harry fired, savagely, and this time he took aim first. At the identical second the python swung its head again and the bullet missed. Harry came nearer, his dissolute mouth trembling— Again he fired, and this time he succeeded. The .38 tore clean through the python's head and it lashed in a constricting fury. Anjani gasped with pain as his own body caught the sudden tightening of the coils.

Again and again Harry fired, then the hammer clicked uselessly as the bullets became exhausted. But the python was struck, half its dreadful head blown away with the bullets. Anjani still pushed and struggled, his strength reborn as he realised the monster was beaten. It quivered, tightened, relaxed, tightened again, then at last the shattered brain of the reptile gave out. It sagged on its coils and became a twitching mass of skin and muscle.

Anjani, breathing hard now the pressure had ceased, dragged himself free of the coils and stumbled through the undergrowth to where Harry was standing, fiddling with the .38 to reload it.

"You save me," Anjani said, gripping his arm, "I not forget. We rest, then go."

He turned to the vegetation, singled out several big leaves then began to wipe himself down swiftly. This done he sat on a broken tree stump and recovered himself, Harry looking at him intently.

"I—I sort of feel better for that," he said. "I didn't

know I could do it!"

"The jungle," Anjani answered, with something resembling contempt, "no place for—er—coward."

Harry came forward slowly, pausing again a few feet from the white giant. He studied him earnestly in the moonlight.

"By this time," he said, "you've got far enough in grasping English to explain yourself, perhaps. I was going to ask you quite a lot of questions had things gone on normally. Maybe I can ask them now whilst you're recovering."

Anjani shrugged and waited.

"Where do you really come from? Where have you been living these last few years?"

"I have lived in jungle—long as I remember," Anjani replied.

"Alone?" Harry asked incredulously.

"No, with tribe. They—er—help me become man. I not belong to tribe. I roam jungle. I know jungle."

"But you didn't know of this other man who looks like you?"

Anjani thought this out for a moment or two and then shook his head. "I not see. Jungle big place."

"You and he must be twins," Harry pointed out. "That means brothers, identical. How do you account for it?"

Anjani shrugged his huge shoulders and got to his feet.

"We not stay here," he said. "Come!" Anjani indicated that Harry should climb on his back. "We go!"

CHAPTER FOUR
ANJANI TO THE RESCUE

A mile to the south of where Anjani and Harry were taking to the trees, a band of Banwui tribesmen led by M'Untino the witchdoctor was on its way through the jungle, following a distinctly visible trail, pursuing in fact the trail made by Tocoto as he had fled through the jungle with Rita.

The delay with the python, however, and Harry's weight, were both deterrents to Anjani's speed, and long before he caught up with his double, Rita, and Caleb Moon, the warriors had come upon them, plodding through the tangle of vines, trees, and elephant grass, the woman queerly dressed in leaves and shoes of vegetation and the trader swinging a rhino-whip in his hand in readiness to deal with any slackness on the part of the natives around him.

Swiftly M'Untino deployed the warriors he had brought with him, and in consequence the three travellers suddenly found themselves surrounded by fantastic natives, all of them still in the paint and regalia of the sacrificial dance from which they had hurried. They formed into a tight little circle, the witchdoctor well to the fore.

"You did not escape so easily, white man," he said, in his own Banwui tongue.

"Escape?" Tocoto repeated in surprise. "What nonsense is this, wise one? I am Tocoto the Mighty, lord of the Banwui!"

M'Untino shook his head. "We followed your trail, white man. You escaped from the sacrificial dance and will return to it in readiness for tonight. We have seen no sign of Tocoto in our travels, so you must be the double of which he told us."

"This man *is* Tocoto," Moon insisted, looking uneasily about him. "Surely you recognise him?"

"No," M'Untino answered blandly, after he had interpreted the trader's faulty language.

"But—*look* at him!" Moon insisted. "He has the scar on the arm which only Tocoto has. He—"

"This is not Tocoto," the witchdoctor answered, and made a signal to his warriors. Immediately Tocoto, Moon, and Rita found themselves tightly seized. M'Untino grinned a little to himself.

He knew perfectly well that this was Tocoto—and so did the warriors, but they did not dare challenge the wisdom of the crabbed old devil who had been given power in their lord's absence. M'Untino, in fact, was enjoying himself thoroughly. For the first time he had a chance to dispose of the white giant legitimately without arousing the ire of the tribe. And then he, M'Untino, would remain as their master. For too long the white man had controlled, and it was because he *was* white that the witchdoctor was so bitterly jealous of him. As for the Jewel of Akada, with its power to master every tribe in the Dark Continent—that could wait. M'Untino's immediate concern was to dispose of Tocoto. It was a chance accidentally thrown in his lap by the escape of Tocoto's double, and it was the thought of him perhaps appearing on the scene at any moment that suddenly got the witchdoctor on the move.

"We return," he announced. "Hurry! Hurry!"

He waved his skinny arms urgently, and the natives did as he ordered. Rita cast a look at the sweating trader as she was bundled along through the midst of the trees, the infuriated Tocoto beside her.

"Isn't there anything you can do?" she asked helplessly, her fear of the tribe far greater than her fear of Moon.

"Nothing. If Tocoto can't stop them, I certainly can't! And I don't like that talk about a sacrifice. If we get tangled up in a fetish like that, it's the finish."

Rita said no more. She was too scared for one thing, and too tired for another. Ever since she had been snatched from the tent the previous night, she had been on the move and, in the slowly increasing heat of the African morning, it was as much as she could do to keep going at all.

Presently she began to stumble, and finally dropped in her tracks. Tocoto made no move to help her and neither did Moon. It was one of the warriors who lifted her in his ebony arms and bore her through the vegetation as if she were a child.

All of which had been witnessed from a height of perhaps twenty feet. Harry slid gently from Anjani's broad shoulders as the giant came to a halt. For the last five minutes he had been following the party below as it hacked its way through the foliage. Now he remained crouched on a broad limb, parting a screen of leaves to peer below.

"It's them, all right," Harry said urgently. "Rita, that fat swine of a Moon, and the man who looks like you."

"He much like me," Anjani admitted. "I not understand," he continued. "They have been captured. Perhaps man who looks like me is supposed to *be* me."

"Perhaps. Anyway, what can we do? We've got to get Rita if we can't grab off the rest."

Anjani considered, then he shot out a hand and stopped Harry as he levelled his .38 through the trees.

"No," he murmured. "You kill one man, two men, then all finish. No, we follow." He signalled silence.

"But what good will that do?" Harry demanded, anxious for Rita, "It's obvious they are captives, and when the native village is reached, they'll probably be killed."

Anjani shook his head. "Tonight danger. Not now. Come—we follow."

As the party below was already moving out of sight in the verdure, Anjani got swiftly on the move, but he soon had to pause as Harry, completely unable to make flying leaps from tree to tree, was left stranded. Once again he finished up on the giant's back. And he was glad of it. The heat of the day was furious now, and his exhaustion almost complete. He realised as he half-drowsed on Anjani's back that he was still a long way from being a fit man.

Anjani continued his progress until at last he came within sight of a native village through the trees. Here he stopped, high in the tree nearest the stockade, and lowered Harry from his back.

"We wait," he said, and fixed himself comfortably in a fork of the tree so he could see and yet not be seen.

Harry settled on a neighbouring limb, his back against the tree bole. He breathed hard and drew the back of his shirtsleeve over his streaming face.

"Sure this is where they'll come to?" he asked.

"Only village," was Anjani's simple response. "And see—sacrificial god still there. This is same village where I was last night. The fire ashes remain."

Harry looked over the high wall of the stockade towards the blackened ground in the distance, then he turned and looked sharply leftwards at sounds from below. The file of natives led by M'Untino was just appearing, the whites in their midst. He and Anjani watched them enter the village, then finally the three were thrust into a grass-and-mud hut, and the warriors broke up and drifted away, one remaining on guard with his spear beside him. M'Untino went over to his own hut and disappeared within it. From the deceptive peace which fell over the area in the shimmering sunlight, nothing might ever have happened.

"I find food," Anjani said abruptly, rising from the fork.

"And leave Rita there? She must be dying of thirst. She was being carried, so that shows she's unconscious. She—"

Anjani pointed to the sun and shook his head. "Not now," he interrupted. "When sun go."

He took a flying leap into the next tree and disappeared. Harry remained where he was, rubbing his sloping chin and trying to decide if there was anything he could do. Then he decided against it. He felt too sick and weak for one thing, and, faced by black warriors, he knew he would stand no chance.

He must leave everything to Anjani and let him handle it. He thought how wonderfully and how quickly Anjani was learning English. It was hardly credible.

After perhaps fifteen minutes, Anjani returned, carrying on one arm a number of melon-like objects. Settling down on the tree branch, he forced a hole in the end of two of them and handed one across. Harry nodded gratefully and drank the sweet juice that poured into his mouth. Then Anjani cracked the fruit apart with his powerful hands and revealed an interior similar to that of a coconut. By the time he had finished eating and drinking, Harry felt considerably better. He only wished to could find some way to get fruit to Rita, but that was out of the question. No possible move could be made until nightfall.

"You say," Harry remarked, as Anjani carefully considered the village and ate at the same time, "you know where Akada is?"

Anjani nodded.

"But are you sure? Can you be absolutely certain that you can reach it? If you are not, then the moment my wife is freed I wish to return to the coast—to Port Durnford."

Anjani looked puzzled, and Harry sighed.

"Of course, I'm forgetting. It's a thousand miles out of your territory. But maybe Rita and I could make it if you could get some natives to help us."

"You not want Akada now?" Anjani asked in surprise.

"Certainly I want it, especially since it seems to have the gold and ivory Moon spoke of, and which you have mentioned. I can sell that stuff and make this hellish trip worthwhile for Rita and myself. But if there is any uncertainty, and you *don't* completely know your way, then I quit."

"Many times sun pass since I got to Akada," Anjani mused. "I maybe...I go there—but jungle not always the same."

"Which means you're not certain?" Harry's expression became one of resignation. "Very well, if we can get Rita free, perhaps you'll set us on our homeward journey. When I get back to Port Durnford, I'll report having met you and see if something can't be done to release you from this wild and dangerous life."

Anjani smiled and shook his head. "I happy here. No wish to go, and I must fight other man like me. He bad man."

"You mean kill your own brother?" Harry asked, astonished.

"He enemy," Anjani replied, evidently quite oblivious the meaning of a flesh-and-blood tie. Then he added: "You and Rita go Akada, and I go too. I take map from trader. Then we find Akada."

Harry gave a start of surprise. "Why yes, that would be a way of making sure. But even then, I don't know. We have no provisions, no tents, no—"

"Your camp still there," Anjani interrupted, pointing back into the jungle. "We go after rescue when moon come. Then go Akada."

Harry was silent for a moment, then: "And what about Moon? Are you going to release him too, when you save Rita?"

"He enemy. I kill him—and white man who look like me."

Which seemed to be the end of the matter. Entirely satisfied with the plans he had in mind, Anjani relaxed against the tree bole and began to doze. With swiftness of an animal he was asleep, yet somehow poised alert and ready for instant action. Harry looked at him in envy and wondered if the amenities of civilisation were so useful after all when the natural life could bring such detachment of mind and body.

But, presently, he too succumbed to the beating heat of the African day. Worn out with his exertions and natural lassitude, he slumbered heavily. To his surprise, when he was awakened by a shaking at his shoulder, it was night again and a coolness had come upon the jungle. He moved stiffly and massaged a leg dead with cramp.

"They get ready for sacrifice," Anjani murmured, and handed over some of the edible fruit in the light of a waxing fire from the centre of the village, "The drums mean sacrifice. They woke me."

"It is very dark," Harry said.

"The sun has long gone. We have slept."

"And I feel better for it," Harry commented, his eyes on the fire. Then he added: "Well, it's night, and time for us to do something, isn't it?"

"Later. When dance of sacrifice begin."

"Bit it may be too late then!"

Anjani shook his head. "I get white woman. You stay here."

"But—surely you need help?"

Anjani grinned, and there was that certain contempt in the dim light. Harry flushed a little.

"I make rescue by self," Anjani explained. "Must be silent. No gun, No noise."

And with this Harry had to be content. In one way he was not sorry that he would not have to do battle with the savages, but in another he wanted to help Rita and prove he was not quite the coward she believed. He continued watching the fire, then presently the drums started again, their reverberation rolling through the jungle's depths. Around the fire their natives started their capering, shields and spears waving.

At last Anjani stood up, made sure his knife was in his loincloth, and then began to drop silently down the tree. Harry said nothing, watching him go. He saw the dim figure reach the stockade, climb over it with perfect ease, and after that Anjani's movements were lost to sight.

Anjani himself remained for quite a while at the base of the stockade, lying flat and studying the situation. At length he made up his mind, put his knife between his teeth in readiness, and glided through the shadows. By means of dodging between the grass-and-mud huts he kept himself out of sight—but in any case the warriors and other members of the tribe were too busy concentrating on the acceleration of the dance to look behind them. So, gradually, Anjani inched his way towards the weirdly-painted warrior standing on the rim of the onlookers.

Abruptly Anjani sprang, forcing the warrior to the ground and pinning him there, knife at his throat.

"You shout, I kill," Anjani warned him softly, in the tribal tongue.

The man struggled for a moment, baffled by the situation, but he had more sense than to argue with the knife at his jugular.

"You have paints and juices stored for the tribal dance," Anjani continued. "Show me where they are."

The native moved a brawny arm indecisively.

"Lead the way," Anjani ordered, allowing him to get up, but keeping the knife ready. "Keep to the shadows. Hurry!"

The warrior did exactly as he was told, powerless to use his spear, and not being fool enough to try and attract attention from the rest of the tribe who were now some distance away around the blazing fire. As they moved, Anjani glanced towards the distant hut where the three whites were imprisoned. A warrior was dimly visible on guard, weirdly painted like the rest of his fellows.

"There," the native said at length and pointed to a nearby hut of the customary grass and mud.

"Enter it," Anjani snapped, and followed the man into the dark interior. It was a move he should not have made, for the warrior immediately turned on him.

Not quickly enough, however. Anjani saw the head of the man's spear flash round towards him, and he instinctively ducked. The weapon missed him by inches, then he had sprung with the agility of a jungle cat and seized the warrior by the throat, bearing him down to the dry grass floor. The man was powerful, but not strong enough to overcome the steel muscles of the giant white man.

Anjani had no time for ceremony, and even less regard for the life of a single native warrior. He squeezed and crushed with relentless force into the man's throat, stifling his cries and smothering the life out of him. At last he could fight no longer and became still. Anjani rose and looked about him, the reflected flickering glare of the fire his only means of illumination. So far his plan was working correctly.

The native had at least spoken the truth in regard to the hut. In one corner Anjani discovered half a dozen big vessels of baked clay containing the dyes and juices used by the natives for painting themselves before the sacrificial dance. In each was a brush made from an animal's tail. Anjani peered at them, finally selecting the darkest liquid of all, He smeared some of it experimentally on his hand, and it looked as though his hand vanished, so black did it become. It was as he had hoped; it was nutgall juice, ebony black when dry.

Moving to the little doorway to study his hand, he looked up suddenly at an increase in the tempo of the sacrificial dance. There were excited cries, extra noise from the tom-toms, and a general atmosphere of new tension. In a moment or two he saw why. Rita, Caleb Moon, and his own giant counterpart were being dragged into the centre of the compound to three stakes erected close to the sacrificial fire. Each of the whites was held by two warriors, from whom it was impossible to break free. Dancing around the whites, flinging up his arms and uttering shrieking exhortations to the demons of his cult, was the odious M'Untino, the witchdoctor.

Anjani stood watching for a moment, until at length all three whites had been bound firmly to the three stakes facing the blaze. Beyond it the fantastic Mantamiza was illuminated. Anjani's face hardened. Things were moving faster than he had expected. In about fifteen minutes the dance would reach its climax, the stakes would be lifted piecemeal with the captives upon them, and be thrown into the devouring flames.

Anjani began moving fast. Hurrying to the nutgall juice he began to plaster himself with it liberally, using the animal tail brush. The hardest part was his back, but he overcame it by tipping the vessel over his shoulders and allowing the juice to flow down him. In perhaps ten minutes he had completely covered himself in the dye, and it was fast drying. Still moving quickly, he snatched up the feathered headdress from the dead warrior and jammed it over his own blond hair. A few smears round his eyes from the pot of white dye, and the dead warrior's spear in one hand and shield in the other, and he was ready for action. The warmth of the fire and that of his body would rapidly dry the juices, and even if this did not happen quickly enough, the disguise might last long enough for his purpose.

So, looking exactly like one of the warriors, he glided out of hut and, by degrees, edged himself into the sacrificial dance, capering with the rest of the natives and gradually moving towards the stakes where the three were tightly bound.

On his way to the stakes, prancing amidst the swirling blood-lusting natives in their incredible regalia, Ajani came upon M'Untino in the midst of an exhortation to the demons he worshipped. In mid-sentence his shouting ended, and none of the natives noticed. They didn't see the witchdoctor drop to the ground, nor did they notice a knife being withdrawn from his skinny chest. With a half grin to himself, Anjani kept on moving.

He came at last to the stakes and, as he moved and capered, took stock of the captives. The giant white man was standing upright, glaring rank defiance. The fat white man was trying hard to release himself, sweat gleaming on his face, his hair tangled and fallen over his forehead. The woman in her vegetation dress seemed to be only half conscious, her head dropping forward so that the golden hair covered her face, the ropes alone preventing her from collapsing.

Anjani moved first towards the trader and then, imitating the natives, he slapped the white man across the face with stinging force. Moon gulped and swore, and the assembled native still capering around broke into derisive laughter. Anjani whooped and slapped again, but at the same time he lowered his hand and snatched the stiff folded map from Moon's shirt pocket, The trader felt it go and for a moment his amazement was greater than his fear. Why the native should want the map was beyond him.

Anjani knew it was time for the dance to end and for the sacrifices to be made, but that order could only come from the witchdoctor—and with him lying dead the ceremony was likely to be indefinitely delayed. Anjani was fully aware of it, and took care to remain near the stakes, watching the dance.

It came when the main body of the dancers began to move in the direction of the fire. Anjani stayed behind—then he suddenly leapt forward, slashed through Rita's bonds in one sweep of his knife, and caught her slumped body in his arms. For a moment Moon and Tocoto imagined that she was to be borne to the fire, but instead they saw the black "warrior" speed away at a tremendous pace towards the stockade.

"See! See!" Tocoto shouted hoarsely, in the Banwui tongue. "The white woman is stolen! Her captor is not one of you: he is the white giant who escaped— The white giant, painted to look like you! What more proof do you need of the fact that *I* am Tocoto, your lord?"

The natives wheeled in confusion, in a quandary as no order came from the witchdoctor. At about this same moment M'Untino's dead body was discovered, and a howl of rage went up. Tocoto, tensely watching, gathered what the rumpus was about.

"Proof! Proof!" he yelled. "There it is! The white man has killed the wise one—I am Tocoto, your lord! Release me! We must capture the white man and woman before he is too far away!"

The warriors came rushing forward, convinced by now that Tocoto was speaking the truth. They slashed him free.

"What about me?" Moon demanded.

"Release him," Tocoto snapped, and bounded away towards the stockade. Moon, freed, looked after him and then felt at his empty pocket where the map had been. He stood watching the natives on the move, all of them speeding to a spot where Anjani had last been seen with Rita.

Moon, always concerned with himself more than anybody else, thought swiftly. As things stood now, without the map, the only means of reaching Akada had gone. Just how Tocoto would react to that, he did not know. Probably he would kill him when he realised he had been cheated of getting the jewel of Akada. In fact it looked to Moon that the safest course for him was to abandon his entire project and get as far from

Tocoto as possible. He had hardly decided upon this course before he was on the move, heading away from the direction Tocoto and his warriors had taken.

Meanwhile, the exhausted Rita over his shoulder, Anjani had reached the tree in which Harry was hiding. Once Harry's amazement at discovering Anjani was black had passed, he helped to lift Rita to the safety of the branch, then Anjani scrambled up beside him. Through the dense foliage of the tree they watched the excited comings and goings in the village, the movement of flaming torches towards the stockade. Then after a while the natives came hurrying below, looking about them, Tocoto in their midst. Anjani grinned broadly.

Harry did not take much notice. His attention was concentrated upon Rita. Holding her head and shoulders up with one arm he allowed the juice of one of the coconut-like fruits to trickle between her blistered lips. It was obvious she was half dead from thirst, and that the natives had not permitted any water.

After a while she coughed and gulped and began to revive. Dazedly she looked around her, scooping the fallen her from before her eyes.

"Harry!" she whispered, recognising him in the reflected light from the sacrificial fire. "Then—then you managed to save me—"

"No, I'm not that tough," he answered dryly. "Anjani did it. He's right here beside us."

Rita looked towards him. But he held up a hand for silence and murmured a warning in a low voice.

"No talking. Natives will hear."

Rita nodded and began to eat the interior of the fruit as Harry broke it open for her. Down below in the jungle could be heard the shouts of the warriors as they continued their search, and occasionally the deeper tones of Tocoto barking out orders in the Banwui tongue.

"They not find us here," Anjani murmured. "When search has failed, we return to your camp. You take this."

Harry found Moon's map handed to him, as Anjani took it from the thong about his loincloth.

"You got it then?" Harry peered at it in the gloom. "That makes us dead sure of reaching Akada. What about Moon? What happened to him?"

"Not know. Man like me, who has name Tocoto, is free. Maybe trader is too. To us it not matter."

From the sound of things the natives were returning again, so the three became silent once more. Before very long the warriors, cursing amongst themselves in their own language, paused directly beneath the giant tree where their quarry was hiding and continued towards the open gateway of the village. They became visible presently, a rather forlorn-looking file of men with the white man amidst them.

"I no time to kill white man like me," Anjani commented after a while. "Maybe later. I have heard name Tocoto before, but did not know it was him."

At that moment Tocoto hesitated and looked about him. He seemed to be endeavouring to make up his mind about something—and finally he did. He turned, headed away into the jungle, and then disappeared.

"Where do you suppose he's going?" Rita, who was making a rapid recovery, asked.

"We have our own troubles," Harry answered. "How about it, Anjani? Can we move now?"

Anjani considered the village, listened intently to the jungle around him, then finally nodded.

"We go," he assented, "but through treetops for safety. I take you both."

"But—the weight!" Rita protested.

Anjani only smiled, so she sacrificed herself to him and was soon draped over his shoulder. Harry did the same on the other shoulder and, burdened though he was, Anjani moved with sureness. He did not attempt any leaps through space, however. Even he had his limits when weighted down with an extra twenty-two stone or thereabouts.

By degrees, resting at intervals, he covered the distance to where the Perrivale camp lay. It was as apparently as untouched as when it had been left, except for the tent which Anjani himself had brought down in his struggle with the natives.

Dropping to a lower branch he caught the girl in his hands and lowered her to the clearing, then Harry jumped down after her.

"We move," Anjani said, when he had dropped beside them. "Natives may come—no time rest. Must go!"

Harry nodded, and Rita, though she was plainly worn

out, did not raise any audible objections. Anything was better than falling again into the hands of the Banwui, so with Harry she began to assist in the rolling up of the tents and collection of the provisions and various odds and ends. They told Anjani to use some of a small drum of paraffin to wipe the dye from his skin. He was amazed at the result, but detested the smell of it.

In half an hour the three were on their way, fully provided for, and Anjani taking more of the load. Armed with machetes from the kit they hacked a way through a tangled wilderness, not so much following any particular direction at the moment as putting as much distance as possible between themselves and the natives if they decided to pursue.

But no pursuit came, and towards dawn Anjani called a halt. They had reached a clearing where they could pitch camp, rest, and take stock. During this time Rita concentrated on teaching the English language to Anjani; his natural intellect made her task very easy. Anjani was an apt pupil.

CHAPTER FIVE
GORILLA ATTACK

Caleb Moon's idea of making a return trek to home now he had no means of getting to Akada, had definitely been hastily conceived. He realised it now as he pushed his way through the jungle in the dawn light. All night he had been on the move, spared attack by savage beasts or reptiles; but the fact remained that he was lost—completely. Nor had he anything with which to protect himself. The warriors had taken his gun and rhino-whip. The only thing he had was a tough tree branch, an extremely poor weapon against the sudden fury that might spring upon him from the fastness at any moment.

Breathing hard, his tattered khaki drill nearly in rags and sodden with perspiration, he sat down on a tree stump and considered. Then he squinted skywards towards the tangle of foliage through which he could catch a glimpse of the rising sun. That way lay the east. It had seemed simple enough to move in that direction, but such is the jungle it can make a man turn in circles without knowing it.

"You try to escape me, white man?"

With a violent start, which nonetheless had a touch of relief in it, Moon turned sharply. Tocoto, with his scarred arm, was standing not very far away. Presumably he had dropped in complete silence from the trees.

"Escape? No," Moon answered, getting up. "I'm glad to see you. I have no gun and I was wondering what to do."

"You did not follow Tocoto last night when the captives escaped."

"I know. You were too quick for me."

Tocoto reflected, his handsome face grim. He came forward to where the fat trader was standing.

"I do not believe you," he said. "You try to reach Akada by yourself and leave Tocoto behind."

"Nothing of the sort. I tried to follow, and lost myself."

"Then we will go to Akada together, as planned. I followed you through the night. You will not escape me."

Moon spread his hands, his black eyes searching the giant's face.

"We cannot reach Akada," he said. "The map was stolen from me by the man who released the white woman—and I suppose it was your double. Without the map, and the white woman to interpret its signs, I cannot do anything. We shall never get to Akada."

Tocoto pondered; then, "Why is this white woman so needed by you? What does she know about the map that you cannot read?"

"There are hidden signs on it which only she under-stands."

Again Tocoto reflected. Moon eyed him and then added:

"At this moment your double and girl will be on their way to Akada. Not the smaller white man, though, since you say he was speared. As for us, we can do nothing."

"This time I will make no mistake," Tocoto muttered, clenching his fists. "The man who looks like me must be destroyed and the map got back. The woman must be seized to read the signs. Come—we will look for them."

Moon had no alternative. Though he no longer felt safe with Tocoto, whom he was convinced might possibly turn on him when the journey to Akada was ended, he was at least a better proposition at the moment than the jungle. There was also another point worrying the trader. He had no weapons with which to defend himself if Tocoto suddenly turned nasty.

All these thoughts went through his mind as he followed in the rear of the white giant through the tangled screen of vines, creepers, and glorious-hued flowers.

"How do you expect to pick up the trail?" Moon asked at length, drawing his sleeve over his streaming face.

"We return to the Banwui kraal and pick up the trail from there. That will not be difficult."

This, however, involved a journey of over two hours,

with a pause on the way for a meal of fruit and a drink of juice. Tocoto would probably have taken to the tree-tops for speed, only it would have meant leaving the trader behind. He was far too bulky to be carried on the giant's back.

"Even when I get the map—if I do," Moon remarked presently, "I shall have difficulty in following it without my compass." He held out his wrist. "Your blasted tribe took it from me."

"I will get it back," the giant said, and pushed on.

And, ultimately, the journey to the village was completed. With some trepidation Moon followed Tocoto across the compound, but he need not have worried. Tocoto's authority, now M'Untino was dead, was absolute, and the natives were perfectly satisfied to agree that he *was* Tocoto, now the witchdoctor was not in control.

In ten minutes Tocoto had recovered the compass from the wrist of one of the natives, who looked supremely disgusted when his 'bangle' was taken from him. He had also gathered a couple of spears and machete knives, together with bottled water and some mealie-meal. This seemed to take care of everything so he led the way out of the compound again with Moon behind him—but hard though the white giant searched, there was no sign of the trail he was seeking.

Finally he came to a halt in his investigation and pondered.

"We not find trail last night," he said, "No clearer in daylight. Escape must have been made through treetops."

Moon looked up at them doubtfully. "I'm no climber. You go above and I'll keep down here."

Tocoto shook his head firmly. "You will come with me. You are the only chance I have of finding Akada. I will drag you into the trees."

Moon had to submit. Tocoto selected the nearest tree and swiftly climbed to its lowest branches, then hanging on by one hand he reached down the other and Moon felt as though a crane had jerked him upwards. Panting hard he scrambled on to the branch beside the jungle man.

"Follow," Tocoto ordered, and, entirely sure-footed amidst the branches, he started forward.

For Moon the journey thereafter was a nightmare. Unskilled in the art of progressing through the trees, and heavily built as well, he was an aching, sweating wreck at the end of half an hour; but Tocoto allowed no let-up. In fact he was irritated by the time the clumsy white man took to keep up with him.

Moon was feeling certain he could go no further and was on the point of saying so when Tocoto suddenly stopped. He crouched and parted the screen of dense leaves before him.

"We follow the treetop trail correctly," he said. "Look!"

Moon was silent, looking down on two tents. Around them were the usual odds and ends of a camp. The tent flaps were open, and from one of them there suddenly emerged the figure of Harry Perrivale, carrying a small tin cup full of steaming water. He hooked a small mirror on the front of the tent pole and began preparations for a shave.

"Him!" Moon breathed in amazement. "I thought he'd been killed!"

"Warrior made a mistake," Tocoto growled, annoyed, then he said no more as Rita came out of the tent also, carrying a small cooking stove. She set it down and began to light it, then, whilst the flame of the wick levelled, she went across to the second tent and called loudly:

"Anjani! Anjani, it's time for a meal."

Within a few minutes Anjani appeared, lithe and smiling, and began to assist with the preparations.

"What are we waiting for?" Moon demanded, as Tocoto made no moves. "All three of them are there and—"

"With guns," Tocoto interrupted. "Smaller man and the woman carrying guns at her belt. We stand no chance against those and fury of the white giant, too. No, there is a better way. Come with me."

Exhausted and mystified, Moon obeyed. Tocoto travelled for perhaps half a mile, then he dropped to the ground. Moon was about to follow him but Tocoto stopped him.

"Stay there, white man. You may get killed. I will not take that risk."

Puzzled, Moon relaxed—then he started as from Tocoto's mouth there suddenly came a tearing scream, half animal and half human. It went rolling away across the jungle and died away in echoes. Moon had heard that noise before—the challenging cry of a bull ape, but why on earth Tocoto was using it he couldn't understand.

Tocoto looked about him and waited. Nothing happened. Birds flew in sudden fear; smaller animals scuttled into the undergrowth. Then Tocoto roared forth again—and this time there was a response from the jungle. Immediately Tocoto whipped out his knife in readiness—and even he looked surprised for a moment at the result of his cries, Normally, a bull ape would have heard the challenge and come to answer it, his supremacy being threatened, but it was no ape which came rolling on his short legs into the small clearing: it was a full-grown gorilla, fighting fangs bared, a monster who stood a full eight feet in height.

Moon gulped in alarm and immediately climbed up a further twenty feet for safety before he peered below. He then found himself looking at the giant white man who had brought this challenge upon himself. With incredible agility he was dodging the gorilla's wild, man-like rushes, and escaping those frightful arms and slavering fangs. Wherever he had a chance, he dashed in and delivered a stab with his knife, but never in a vital spot. Screaming with the pain of his wounds the gorilla's fury mounted, and he made mighty efforts to seize the lithe white-skinned attacker who was tormenting him.

Then, for a reason that Moon could not understand, Tocoto suddenly turned tail and fled into the jungle.

Instantly the gorilla thundered after him, whipping branches and trees out of his way as he travelled. The trader listened to the dim thunder of pursuit dying away, then he drew his sleeve over his face.

"Crazy," he muttered. "That's what he is. Where's the sense of bringing a damned gorilla to fight you when you can be peaceful?"

But after a moment or two, his hopes began to rise. If Tocoto should be killed by the gorilla, it might be an advantage. A chance would surely come, Moon was convinced, when he could sneak into the enemy camp and get the map for himself. He was armed and provisioned now, and could carry on by himself if need be—yes, perhaps it was better this way.

"An old jungle trick," said the voice of Tocoto, and with a start Moon turned. The white giant was just appearing through the trees, completely unhurt, a hard grin on his face.

"You—you escaped, then?" Moon asked despondently.

"I *meant* to escape. Umnuzi, the mighty one, will look for me—and find the man who looks like me."

Gradually the plan began to dawn on Moon.

"You—you mean you deliberately goaded that gorilla and then gave him the slip, so that he'll attack your double instead?"

Tocoto nodded. "I ran to the edge of the camp and then leapt into a tree. Umnuzi went straight on, and will attack the other man who looks like me. Umnuzi hunts by sight, not scent. I did not stay to see what happened. I keep you beside me— But come, we will look."

In truth many things were happening in the Perrivale camp at this moment. The wounded gorilla, roaring in fury, burst upon them before they realised it, though for some time beforehand Anjani had been alerted by the noise of the beast coming nearer.

As the shaggy monster with his terrible fangs came blundering in view, Rita screamed and dived into the tent for safety. Harry swung round, half-shaven, and dropped his razor, his hand flying to his gun. Before he could snatch it out, the enraged beast had struck him across the face with terrific force. It sent the hapless man spinning a dozen yards to crash into the under-growth with a broken jaw and his senses reeling.

Anjani jumped warily to one side as the gorilla thundered on towards him. Then, doubling back, the white man landed a killing blow straight in the beast's stomach, increasing his howls of rage. By this time Anjani had his knife out and, prancing cautiously, he watched for a chance to strike. Whilst he did so, Rita came out of the tent again, a rifle to her shoulder. She took aim courageously, and fired. The bullet gashed the gorilla's chest and with a scream of rage he swung round and plunged at the puny woman a few yards away.

What would have happened to her Rita did not dare to think—had not the spiked top of the tent pole saved her. In his furious rush forward the gorilla failed to notice it, until it drove like a spear in his stomach and jolted him to a stop. In blind anger he snapped the pole away, ripped the canvas of the tent into shreds and overturned the lighted oil stove with his raging feet. Instantly flame spewed along the course grass and seized on the canvas wreckage.

Saved from injury so far, Rita ran blindly, her only chance, straight into the jungle. Without realising it she was still clinging to the rifle and had a cartridge belt slung across one shoulder.

Probably the gorilla would have followed her, but a flaming faggot, impelled by Anjani, checked him and he went to deal with the white man. It was sheer bad luck that Harry chose at that moment to get up from the undergrowth and stagger forward in an effort to help. The gorilla sighted him out of the corner of his bloodshot eyes, swung left, and seized the running man in his mighty hands.

Nothing could save Harry Perrivale then. He was swung high in the air like a rag doll and dashed with merciless fury against the bole of a nearby tree. Anjani watched in horror as the thing that had been a man was battered to a smashed and bleeding pulp. He was thankful that Rita had escaped and not seen her husband's ghastly fate.

Then, satisfied for the moment, and becoming increasingly alarmed by the fire, the gorilla flung away the mutilated corpse and bared his fangs at Anjani. Anjani crouched, legs tensed ready to spring, knife in his right hand. He waited until the gorilla lunged, then he too sprang, straight up, seizing the shaggy hair with one hand and driving the knife straight into the barrel of a chest where lay the fierce heart. The monster squirmed and twisted to pull the white tormentor free, but doing that only tugged his own hair and gave him fresh pain. With his legs scissored round the gorilla's middle, Anjani hung on, just below the brutal head so he could not be bitten by the fighting fangs any more than a man can bite something immediately under his chin.

But the gorilla had a dim sense of reason somewhere in its savage brain. Torn with anguish from the repeated blows of the knife, it locked its mighty arms about the white man and bore him to a tree as far as possible from the flame that was fast gaining a hold.

Anjani jolted and gulped with pain as his back was slammed hard against the tree. The force of it felt as though it had smashed his spine. He wriggled and struggled with his tremendous muscles and, very slightly, the shaggy arms relaxed their grip. He withdrew his knife from the enormous, bleeding chest in front of him and stabbed instead at the forearms locked around him.

The gorilla howled, but did not let go. Instead it retaliated with blinding blows to Anjani's head and face, and at the same time battered him hard against the tree. He gulped and coughed, his lungs torn by crushed bone. With a final last effort, as he felt his senses going, be brought up his knife and drove it with all his power straight into the gorilla's eye.

That did it, the long blade piercing the brain. With

a gasping cry the brute fell forward, pinning Anjani with its huge dead weight. Crushed and injured, Anjani fought inch by inch to tear himself free, given a final strength by the knowledge that the flames consuming the clearing were now not very far away from him.

He dragged away, coming almost immediately on something that crackled in his hand. He took it for a leaf until he looked at it, then he realised it was the map of the route to Akada which must have been jolted from Harry Perrivale's pocket when he had been slain.

With an effort Anjani pushed it safely below the thong of his loincloth and then crawled away in the bushes. He knew the fire would probably reach him before long, but he had to rest. The whole world was spinning before his eyes—then it seemed the whole world had completely collapsed at that very moment, for he went flying down into a dusty emptiness and landed with an impact that knocked the remaining senses out of his twisted body.

And, high above the blazing clearing, Moon and Tocoto looked at one another. They had witnessed the whole terrifying act from start to finish, and now the view was obscured by smoke.

"Seems to me you were too thorough," Moon said sourly. "Perrivale, who probably had the map, has been smashed to a jelly, and he and the map will be burned to a crisp in this fire."

"Woman escaped into jungle," Tocoto said impassively. "Tocoto saw her go. We will find her. She has seen the map many times and can tell us. Come."

Moon hesitated, then he began to follow Tocoto through the treetops, skirting the edge of the rapidly gaining holocaust and finally coming beyond it with the smoke wreaths blowing to the rear.

And while the two men searched for her, Rita herself was in the midst of the jungle, trying frantically to find a way through the barrier of flame sweeping ever nearer. Her lungs were filled with smoke, and she coughed desperately in between calling out the names of Harry and Anjani. When neither responded, she began to fear the worst and searched desperately for some way to get back to the camp she had left—but there was none. In all directions the fire was sweeping and devouring, coming ever closer—

She was compelled to move further and further away from the inferno, and as she went she was constantly startled by animals of all shapes and sizes bounding across her path. She saw two lions amongst them and felt her blood freeze, but the jungle monarchs were too alarmed for their own safety to pay any attention to her. Fire, the dreaded enemy of all animals, was on its relentless way.

Dazed, convinced she was running in circles, nearly overcome by the heat of the flames and the sun, Rita went on blindly through vine, thicket, and elephant grass. She had the feeling that if she could only get beyond the rim of the flames, she might be able to make a detour—but in this she revealed her lack of knowledge of a forest holocaust. Now it had got really started, it would continue blazing in all directions until rain extinguished it—which did not seem very likely at the moment—or it came to a wide stream or river which killed its further advance.

The more she realised this inevitable fact, the more Rita had to pin her hopes on the thought that Anjani, with his skill in jungle tracking, would find her later. So she blundered on, hardly daring to pause for a moment in case the flames encircled her and she found herself fatally trapped....

Of the rustling and disturbance overhead she took no notice, believing they were caused by birds and monkeys on the move—until she was brought to a stop by a white giant leaping down to the tangled vegetation in front of her. For one wild moment of relief she thought it was Anjani, then she recognised the scarred arm and loincloth, the hardness of the features.

In two strides Tocoto had come forward and gripped her arm. She tried uselessly to pull away, then she stopped and her eyes moved to Moon as he scrambled down from the trees and came over to her.

"Apparently we are destined to travel with each other, Mrs. Perrivale, whether we like it or not," he commented. "For my own part, I *do* like it—very much."

Rita wrenched her arm free and made to snatch her rifle from under her other arm, but Tocoto was too fast for her. He took the weapon and cartridges and handed them to Moon.

"You will find these useful perhaps," he said, and Rita wished desperately that she could understand the tongue Tocoto used.

"We move—quickly," Tocoto said, with a glance at the smoke columns rising high. "The river is not far away. Come."

"You should be grateful that we decided to follow you, Mrs. Perrivale," Moon told her. "Both your husband and the double of Tocoto here are out of the running. Your husband is dead, in fact, but I'm not sure about—"

"Dead?" Rita repeated, her eyes wide in horror. "No! No, I don't believe it! You said that once before and you were quite wrong."

"This time there is no mistake. The gorilla that went berserk in your camp battered him to a pulp. I am a pretty hardened man but it took me all my time to watch. As to the white man, I doubt if he will survive the fire. He was trying to crawl away from it when Tocoto and I last saw him. He was pretty badly hurt, I think."

Rita went on dully through the tangled wilderness, her mouth drooping. Moon looked at her again.

"By yourself, you could not have survived," he said.

"I would rather have died than be forced to go with you and—and this twin of Anjani's," Rita retorted.

"Ask the white woman about the map," Tocoto ordered, and Moon nodded.

"We are heading for Akada, Mrs. Perrivale," he said, "My map was taken from me, as you're aware, so I have no means of finding my way. You probably studied the map a good deal with your husband and can remember its main points."

Rita gave a wondering glance. "But you had the map far longer than we did! You surely must remember every point that it indicated? I certainly don't!"

The trader grinned. "I remember most of it, certainly, but two heads are better than one in this case. With your memory and mine we ought to find our way. That's why we decided to try and find you again.... At least that was one reason."

Rita was in no doubt what Moon meant, and her eyes became stonily contemptuous.

"Both of us are permitted to go on living, I think, because Tocoto believes we know the way to Akada," Moon added. "He must go on thinking that. You cannot say anything to him in any case because you do not speak his language. As I remember it, we travel eastwards to the cliff shaped like a demon's ear, then bear north to a plateau where, fifteen miles distant, there stands a three-peaked mountain range. Beyond it is Akada. Yes, I think we might find the way. Fortunately, I have recovered my compass."

Rita glanced at it on his wrist and said nothing. Words seemed totally inadequate to deal with the situation. She still had not got over the terrible fact that her husband had been killed—if Moon had spoken the truth. Knowing he had been wrong on the previous occasion, she still hoped dimly that he had repeated the mistake. As for Anjani, if he too were dead, then the position was hopeless as far as she was concerned. She was under no illusion regarding the trader's intention towards her. At the moment it was only Tocoto who stood in the way of the trader's lust.

CHAPTER SIX
ORDEAL OF THE CROCODILES

Anjani stirred slowly, and then relaxed again. He coughed, and every cough was like the turning of a knife blade in his lungs. He felt he could not move a single muscle. For a long time he lay with his eyes closed, trying to pick up the threads of broken consciousness. Then he remembered—The gorilla, the slaughter of Harry Perrivale, the onrushing fire.

His eyes opened, looking upwards to a baobab hut roof thatched in tukula leaves and underlined with dried mud. A dim light was flickering nearby, an improvised lamp made of gut and animal oil and fixed in a crude clay container.

Nothing seemed to fit properly in Anjani's mind. His last remembrance was of falling inwards to darkness. And now he was on rough bed of raffia, tortured by the pain of crushed bones and numberless lacerations. By degrees, however, he realised that the lacerations had been smeared with a cooling ointment. Somebody, then, had befriended him.

Weakly, he called for help. Immediately a native appeared in the hut doorway—having evidently been just outside it. He looked at Anjani for a long moment, then turned and hurried away. Shortly afterwards, he returned with a woman of his tribe—a fat, chocolate-brown woman who at some time had evidently mixed with white blood somewhere. She moved quickly to the bed and went on her knees. In the doorway more natives crowded, falling apart as a much older member of the race, grey-haired and withered, came creeping in.

Anjani took one look at him and his eyes widened.

"Miambo," he whispered. "Miambo, it is you!"

"Yes, Anjani. It is Miambo. You lie still. You still much hurt. Limina tend your wounds."

Anjani relaxed again, trying to fathom what miracle had put him into the care of the tribe who had reared him from babyhood. In the course of his life, he had mingled with many tribes, but his main affection was for this particular one—the Untani, peaceable folk who were much advanced from the savages who worshipped Mantamiza and who indulged in sacrificial rites. Perhaps this was because Miambo, ruler of the tribe, was an old man of uncommon wisdom who believed more in signs and wonder than the ruthless law of the spear and the flame.

Anjani stirred again as Limina—who had been a mere slip of a girl when he had last seen her—tended his wounds. He looked towards the impassive Miambo.

"Miambo, wise one, how came I here? I remember crawling into the elephant grass, then I fell—down, unto some kind of pit...."

"You fell into a lion-snare, my son. We have many of them about the kraal, as you know. Because of that the fire passed over you. We, in destroying the fire by cutting down the vegetation before it could reach us, came upon you and brought you here. Now rest...."

"Yes, Anjani, rest." Limina murmured, looking in wondering admiration at his massive body. "Limina will watch over you."

In spite of his pain Anjani gave a half smile. Even as a girl Limina had always cast eyes upon him. Being, by some unexplained mystery in her ancestry, partly white herself, she had considered herself more than worthy of his favours—until his roaming tendencies had taken him away from the tribe. But now he was back, and she was a full-grown woman. Her hand passed softly over his forehead.

"I—I must mend quickly," he said, glancing about him at the faces. "I have much to do. A white woman lost in the jungle needs my protection. She may even be in the hands of a man who looks like me."

Limina's hands moved away from Anjani's forehead and a glint of jealousy came into her eyes.

"Man who looks like you?" Miambo repeated gravely. "You mean Tocoto the Mighty?"

"I do, wise one. Lord of the Banwui tribe."

"He your brother, my son," Miambo said. "I never told you that. I did not see what good it could do you. Now you must know. The great gods say it is evil to kill one's own brother, or any that belongs by flesh and blood."

"The great gods also say that an enemy must be slain. He is my enemy, and the enemy of the white woman. She is unable to defend herself. She relies completely on me—and this. This she must have."

With an effort Anjani pulled the map he had found from his loincloth and held it open. Then he returned it to safety.

"There is also another," he added. "A fat white man who brings no good to the white woman. I hope he may be dead, but I do not think so. Tocoto is his friend—and my enemy."

"You wish to mate with this white creature?" Limina asked bluntly.

Anjani turned his eyes to her. "She is white, Limina, as I am. Her mate is dead—killed by Umnuzi when he burst into our camp...." Anjani stirred restlessly, only to be forced back by the pain of his wounds. "I must go," he repeated feverishly. "I must...."

"You will not go anywhere just yet," Miambo decided with finality. "You have the fever. I will dispatch warriors to look for this white woman. You rest. Limina, you will watch over him."

The girl nodded, but not with particularly good grace. Miambo turned to the men around him and gave orders, then as they went out he moved to the side of the bed and went on one knee.

"My son, you have never known how you came to be amongst us," he said. "I will tell you this now, so that Limina—who has always wanted you for her mate—can know the truth.... You listen, my son? You are not too tired?"

"I listen," Anjani assented, his eyes closed.

"Many moons ago, when I was far younger than now and had just come to rulership of the Untani, I was engaged on a jungle expedition and came upon a deserted camp. There was one white man dead, a spear through his body. In the camp were two tiny white babies. We took them. Upon our return home, we were attacked by the Banwui tribe. They stole one of the babies and we kept the other.... That other became you. You waxed strong. We and the Banwui are separated by many marches and did not cross each other's paths again. Which is why you did not meet your brother, though I learned he had been named Tocoto the Mighty and become leader of his tribe.... When you left us, I knew you could take care of yourself, so I said nothing. The white man we found dead must have been your father. Of the mother there was no sign.

"One day we decided to examine that camp again. When we got there we found an expedition exploring. All that remained of the one-time man was clean-picked bones. I had remembered he had certain strange parchments in his pocket, which, at the time, I had not been able to take because of the Banwui attack. Those parchments were now gone. The expedition had taken them. I believe, my son, that the parchment you have just shown me may have belonged to your father and it has been handed down—so you, by the law of the gods, are its rightful owner. You are not of us, my son. You are white, pure white. You, Limina, are partly black. You and Anjani can never mate. I forbid it, and the gods forbid it."

"Yes, wise one," Limina acknowledged quietly, knowing that Miambo's edict was absolute.

"I did not realise," Anjani murmured, "that I was so near my own beloved tribe when Umnuzi attacked, otherwise I should have called for help."

Miambo stood up and laid his hand for a moment on Anjani's hot forehead.

"Rest, my son," he said. "If the woman can be found, my warriors will do it."

Anjani had no choice, since he was too ill to move anyway, but the warriors who set out to find Rita were unlucky. Good bush trackers though they were, most of the trail Rita, Tocoto, and Moon had created had been destroyed by the now departed fire—which had moved several miles northward—leaving no clue behind.

In actual fact, Rita, Tocoto, and the trader were many miles away by this time, still moving rapidly to escape the fire that pursued them. Their chance came when the jungle thinned suddenly ahead and they found themselves on the banks of a swift flowing river.

"We cross," Tocoto said, and put his knife in his teeth.

"What's the knife for?" Moon demanded—but Tocoto did not answer the question. Rita pointed suddenly to something like a tree trunk appearing out of the water and then submerging again.

"Crocodiles!" she gasped in horror. "What does he expect us to do? Swim?"

"I can't swim anyway," Moon answered, with a backwards glance towards the fire, not very far away.

Apparently, though, Tocoto had no intention of swimming. His knife still in his teeth he seized the lowest branch of a nearby tree and bent and twisted it until it gave way. Then he used the knife to strip it of leaves. He motioned quickly as Moon and Rita stood watching him.

"Hurry!" he told the trader. "We make raft. Time short."

The two jumped into action at that, preservation of themselves the only thought. The still advancing fire was sufficient goad to make them work non-stop. Under Tocoto's directions a small raft was made, bound together with vine and creeper, and three long sticks were selected for 'punting.'

"We go to other side," Tocoto said at length. "You have the gun," he added to the trader. "Use it. The white woman will help me push the raft. Come."

With the fire to the rear there was no choice, so the raft was heaved into the fast-flowing water, and the three jumped upon it, Moon with the rifle to his shoulder in readiness.

The pull of the current was tremendous, and Rita knew that, alone, she would never have been able to hold the clumsy craft against its surging had it not been for Tocoto. He, with his immense strength, and obviously accustomed to mastering a powerful river, kept the raft broadside to the current, and heading towards the opposite bank.

It was in mid-stream when trouble came. Crocodiles, moving with the river, became inquisitive concerning this weird object in their midst. Some of them braced themselves against the crudely fashioned branches and opened their cavernous mouths to bite at it. One, indeed, did snap a corner from the raft. But the next time its mouth opened, a bullet slammed into it and the monster slid away in a dark welter of blood.

Then, when only perhaps twenty yards from the opposite bank, real disaster came. A crocodile heaved up underneath the raft and tipped them all off. Rita found herself plunging into the fast-swirling water and Moon landed beside her. Around them, sweeping rapidly in their direction with the current, came the crocodiles.

"It's the finish!" Moon babbled, struggling helplessly since he could not swim. "They'll get us—"

He went under, his hands waving. Rita, fighting for herself, twisted around and struck out for the bank—then she paused and looked desperately around her as a crocodile barred the way. It dived suddenly and she waited in an agony of apprehension, knowing that if the monster chose to come up beneath her, its steel-trap jaws could bite her body in half an instant.

But she had reckoned without Tocoto. She caught a glimpse of him as a mighty arm flashed in the water, then his feet momentarily appeared as he dived down into the depths. He came up again in a second or two, his hands holding apart the jaws of the crocodile Rita had seen heading towards her. Perfect swimmer though he was, Tocoto had no need to swim at this moment; the crocodile kept him floating since he had locked his legs over the creature's scaly back.

Rita absorbed this amazing sight of the white man endeavouring to break the hinges of the monster's jaws, then she remembered Moon. He was not far away, being carried by the current, his forearms locked over the edge of the raft which had caught up with them. He was making frantic efforts to get a leg onto the raft and haul himself up but, so far, the speed of the current had stopped him.

Then as he saw a second crocodile coming towards him, he redoubled his efforts. Rita saw the monster coming too, and it was much nearer her than Moon. She would inevitably be the first to be attacked. There was nothing Tocoto could do. He was riding the monster nearby, his mighty arms pulling with ever-increasing tension to rip the terrible jaws apart.

Rita twisted round and struck back towards the raft to which Moon was clinging. His eyes were fixed in goggling horror on the incoming reptile. Rita, however, had seen that on the raft there still lay the rifle that had been jolted from Moon when he had overbalanced. Whether she could ever take aim on the raft's pitching surface Rita did not know, but she was willing to try.

Being far less in weight than Moon and much more agile, she managed to scramble onto the raft and put the rifle to her shoulder—but her two shots went hopelessly wide. To take dead aim was impossible, so instead she squatted with the weapon vertical in her hands, watching the monster come towards her. She waited until the moment when it opened its mouth, then she put the rifle upright in the extended jaws and flung herself back.

Moon had seen a few courageous acts in the course of his dubious career, but few the equal of this. For Rita had definitely stopped this particular attacker in its tracks. It could not close its jaws. For all its vast mandible power, it could not break the steel barrel and hard wood of the rifle. It was completely gagged, and the more pressure it exerted, the more it pained itself as steel and wood gouged into the roof and base of its mouth. Fighting with itself, jaws extended, it went sailing down the river.

At about the same time Tocoto gave a final mighty wrench and won his own struggle with the monster he was fighting. Its jaws broken, blood staining the water from the fractured ligaments, the crocodile went writhing and struggling away.

"Get—get me up," Moon panted, as Rita lay near him, nearly exhausted with reaction and fatigue. "One of these blasted things may bite the legs off me any minute."

She struggled towards him and wondered, even as she tried to haul him into the raft, why she was doing it. She had nothing to thank Moon for, and would probably have even less in the future, yet the woman in her insisted she could not leave him to possible ghastly death. Heaving and pulling, she locked her arms under the trader's and dragged with all her strength. Wet and gasping, he managed to drag his feet up and lie flat beside her. Before he could say anything, Tocoto had swiftly swum the distance to the raft and swung aboard it.

"River narrows ahead," he said. "Low-growing trees. We will catch a branch and swing free. Otherwise we shall be caught in the waterfall."

He stood up, keeping his balance, and watching for further crocodile attacks—but at this point the river had gained such an impetus no crocodiles attempted anything. In fact, none of them were visible at this point, probably knowing that the river was heading for the edge of a high cliff over which it would soon plunge,

Tensely, Rita and Moon watched for what was to happen next. The raft, with no poles to guide it, was quite uncontrollable—and presently, from far ahead, there came the growing thunder of water tumbling into a deep gorge,

"If he isn't right about overhanging trees, it's the finish for us," Moon muttered, glancing at the girl.

She turned to him, puzzled. "What trees?"

"I forgot: you don't understand his language. He says we grab the trees overhead when they span the river, as they will do soon. Our only chance. I only hope he isn't wrong."

Tocoto, though, was not wrong. He knew the jungle geography too well for that. Presently, as the sound of the falls became a real and deafening roar, the banks of the river closed inwards abruptly, bringing the foliage on the opposite banks nearly within touching distance—and in another minute or so the tree branches had actually interlocked.

Tocoto straightened, reached upwards, then swung himself aloft. Rita did likewise, Moon hanging on the same branch as herself as the raft shot from beneath them and was gone. They hung over the raging torrent—but whereas Moon had the masculine power to pull himself upwards and gain safety, Rita was left dangling, her fingers dying slowly from cramp.

Moon seemed to think for a moment, then making up his mind, he fixed himself securely and leaned downwards, locking his arms about her. By degrees, flinging her feet upwards, she managed to gain a grip on the tree branch with her knees—and with Moon to help her to finish the job, she finally reached a secure position. Breathing hard, she pushed back her soaked hair from her face.

Moon, poised in the fork of the branch, considered her. She knew she was practically stripped of clothing. Her vegetation garment had gone, as had her shoes. All that remained were a few tattered vestiges of her original shorts and silk blouse. For some reason, she felt that she did not particularly care at the moment. She was tasting the delightful reaction of having looked death in the eyes and escaped.

"That makes us quits," Moon said finally, and, still struggling to regain her breath, Rita looked at him in surprise.

"Quits? How do you mean?"

"I mean that you saved my life on the raft, and I saved yours just now. That puts us back where we started. I shall not feel I'm under an obligation...later."

Rita looked at him bitterly. "I should have left you to drown. You just can't get over the fact that I'm a woman, can you?"

"As you are now, I find it even more difficult," Moon replied; then he glanced behind him as, with a rustling of leaves, Tocoto appeared. He looked first at the trader, then at the girl, and nodded in satisfaction.

"Tocoto glad that you survive," he said. "Tocoto did not save you because he is your friend, but because only you and the white woman can find the way to Akada. We continue our journey—"

"Not before we've rested," Moon snapped. "What do you think we're made of? Let's get down to the bank and stop for a while. We've pretty well lost everything we had, but we can get some fruit and juice to survive on."

"Very well," Tocoto agreed. "Maybe we should make camp.... We are off the beaten track," he added. "Can you still find the way to Akada?"

Moon hesitated, his eyes straying to his waterlogged and useless compass. Without it, even though he had memorised the map directions, he did not see how he was possibly going to keep on the right course. Yet if he admitted he was beaten—a fact made even more certain by having moved several miles because of the river—there was a chance Tocoto would instantly kill him off as useless, and in revenge. Had he not said that he had only rescued him and Rita because they could find the way to Akada? If this was not fulfilled, then—

"I asked you a question," Tocoto snapped impatiently. "Can you still find the way to Akada?"

"Uh-huh, I think so," Moon assented. "But let us rest first."

Rita, handicapped by not knowing the tribal language, gave a glance of enquiry, so Moon explained the situation to her.

"And how long do you think you can keep up a deception like that?" she demanded, as they began to move through the treetops after Tocoto.

"Not very long, I'm afraid—but you see the position, If he once suspects we're lost, he'll kill the pair of us. I have only one alternative—to kill him first."

Rita smiled contemptuously as she progressed. "You couldn't. He's too powerful for you."

"I agree. But I shall not be such a fool as to challenge him to a direct fight."

"And if you kill him, what then?" Rita's voice was hesitant. "Just what good would it do? We still would not reach Akada, and you and I would be left."

"Which would be nearly as good as reaching Akada—to me," Moon commented. "While it lasted, anyway."

"You—you fat beast! I—"

Rita stopped as Tocoto glanced in puzzlement over his shoulder. For the time being the matter was closed. Rita knew as clearly as Moon that death *could* be the answer if Tocoto once got suspicious, so she said no more—but she made many plans of her own. When the chance came, she would try and escape. Better to die before the fangs of a jungle beast than be left alone with this horrible trader. With Tocoto she felt safe, hard-natured though he obviously was. He had no use for her beyond the fact that she could, or so he believed, help in guiding the way to the lost city.

In a few more minutes, Tocoto dropped to the ground in a small clearing, and Moon and Rita followed his example.

"We will rest here," he said. "We shall gather fruits—I will show you. Come."

Moon and Rita followed the giant to the surrounding trees, and he pointed out the fruits that could be used. Rita glanced about her, wondering if this was the ideal moment to try and escape—but before she could make up her mind, Tocoto and Moon were facing her again, No, not yet. It would be more sensible to if she gained some rest first—so she coiled herself up in as feminine a matter as possible and accepted the fruit Moon handed down to her, Thereafter, as he sat munching and drinking the juice, he never took his sloe-black eyes from her. She could almost feel her skin crawling.

"We have travelled far," Tocoto commented presently, looking up towards the sky. "The moon is coming. We stay here now and go with the sun tomorrow. We need fire."

He got up and began to busy himself collecting dry brushwood and tinder dust from around the clearing. By patiently spinning a stick in the tinder he produced fire, and after a while a blaze crackled up in the clearing centre. Rita lay watching it absently, too tired to move now she had at last relaxed. Her mind strayed back to Harry, and she still wondered if he had met with the ghastly fate Moon had described.

Moon had taken his eyes from her now, and was apparently also lost in thought. It was dawning upon him how long he had been without his beloved whiskey, and the effect was not at all pleasant. It seemed to have created a perpetual stomach ache, and a temper so brittle it was liable to snap at any moment. But because he had other things to think about, he managed to keep himself more or less under control. In his heart he had entirely given up all hope now of ever reaching Akada. In fact, the possibility was that once he had wiped out Tocoto—as he fully intended in the not too distant future—he would become one more victim of the jungle. Before that happened, though, he and Rita would be alone in the wilderness and that, even if it was destined to be his last earthly pleasure, was worth looking forward to.

In this state of mind he dozed, and fell asleep. Rita, too, lowered her head to her arm and became oblivious. With both herself and Moon, their outraged constitutions needed restoring—but as far as Tocoto was concerned, he remained lounging near the fire, feeding it at intervals, pondering upon the frailty of the two whites upon whom his hopes depended.

But even he was not so superhuman that he did not need sleep and, as the night came and deepened, he dozed at intervals, his senses nevertheless always partly alert, animal-fashion, for any sudden attack. None came, and with the dawn he stirred and stretched into wakefulness, and then went across to shake the trader and Rita back to life.

Both of them were stiff and cramped, but far stronger for the rest. Whilst Tocoto and Moon gathered a breakfast of the unusual monotonous fruit, Rita went to work fashioning another vegetable leaf garment and shoes for herself. By the time the 'breakfast' was over, she felt almost respectable again and still full of the resolve to make a break the moment an opportunity showed.

So the journey into the jungle began again, and this time with extreme slowness, since there were no machetes with which to hack away the vegetation. Danger was also increased by the only weapon being Tocoto's knife. Moon, aware of this, found a short, thick stick for himself and held it in readiness.

It seemed to Rita—and she was right in her judgment—that the present trekking amounted to nothing more than a waste of time and energy. They were just getting nowhere, even though they were bearing roughly east according to the sun. But just the same the journeying continued; the forest was interminable.

By night they always stopped in a clearing and dozed around a fire, then next day they were on their way again. As far as Rita could judge, nearly a week of this kind of monotonous, sweltering progress had been experienced when Tocoto, usually silent, showed the first signs of suspicion.

Suddenly stopping in the midst of the advance through the vegetation, he turned and looked at Moon with a sinister glint in his blue eyes.

"Where do you lead Tocoto?" he asked curtly. "We have travelled great distance, always watching the sun, but we do not see Akada. When does our journey end?"

Moon shrugged, immediately on his guard. "I am doing my best, Tocoto, and so is the white woman. We were taken off course by that river. It is hard to find the way again."

"Tocoto watches you," the giant said. "He does not see you look at the bangle on your arm. You said you must have it to find the way. Are you sure you still *know* the way to Akada?"

Moon smiled uneasily, glancing down at the ruined compass on his wrist. Then he became blusteringly reassuring.

"Certainly we know the way. Any time now. Tomorrow we ought to reach the cliff shaped like a demon's ear."

Tocoto said nothing, but his mouth was hard. At last he turned his back and continued to push on through the jungle with the trader and the girl behind him. Moon fell back so that he came alongside Rita.

"What was all that about?" she questioned. For herself she would much rather have cold-shouldered Moon throughout, but the circumstances were such she just could not do so.

"He's getting suspicious," Moon muttered. "Not that

I'm surprised after a week of hacking through this frizzling hell. If there is no sign of anything tomorrow he'll turn on us: I'm sure of it. So tonight we'll make a break for it."

Rita did not answer. For her, that meant that she must also make a break, and escape, no matter what the consequences—so, until the time came for them to rest, she turned over various ideas in her mind and reached no particular conclusion. At last they came to quite a large clearing in which to camp. Rita made her plans.

Moon, however, had apparently guessed what was in her mind though he said nothing at the time. When it came to the sleeping period, Tocoto dozing by the fire at the base of a tree, Rita forced herself to stay awake, watching for a chance to steal off into the jungle behind her. The night was moonless, so there was little chance of her trail being picked up. She knew survival was probably too much to hope for, but anything was better than being left alone with Caleb Moon.

At last Tocoto was obviously asleep, his head slumped forward, hands dangling over his slightly raised knees. From Moon there came a brief snore. Rita squirmed from under the giant leaves she was using as 'blankets,' and immediately began to glide towards the surrounding screen of jungle that was some way from the clearing. But before she had actually plunged into the dense bushes, there were light footsteps behind her. She spun round just as Moon gripped her arm tightly,

"No, you don't!" he said, breathing hard after his

run. "I thought you'd do something like this, but you're not escaping *me*! We go together—"

Rita lashed out at him, but he easily checked the blow; then, before she knew what was happening, he had a length of tough thong about her wrists and had secured them tightly behind her back. Stooping, he also fastened her ankles together. She half began to scream but a blow across the face silenced her. The next moment, part of part of her silk blouse projecting from the vegetable dress had been thrust into her mouth and secured there with a double length of vine. Luckily for Moon they were too far away for Tocoto to hear them.

"That's better," Moon panted, "I don't want Tocoto chasing after us even if you do. Our main object— mine anyway—is to give him the slip."

With that he lifted her into his arms, wheezing a little under her weight, and began to carry her through the jungle. He could not keep it up for long, and finally put her down again, loosening the thong about her ankles so that she could at least walk.

"Keep moving," Moon snapped. "Tocoto will probably try and follow us when he wakes up, but I'm hoping that by that time we shall be far enough away for the trail to be too confused for him to follow. I suppose I should have killed him, really, but suppose you tell *me* how one can kill a man like that. I'd have been wiped out before I could even get near him. Anyway, he can't start until it's light."

Since Rita was incapable of answering, she kept stumbling onwards, Moon keeping up with her.

"No knife," the trader said at length. "No arms at all. This 'elopement' isn't going to be very comfortable, Mrs. Perrivale!"

CHAPTER SEVEN
THE END OF MOON

During the week in which Rita, Tocoto, and Moon had been on the march, Anjani too had fought for recovery. Two things hastened his convalescence—his all-consuming desire to help Rita, and his iron constitution. The fever rapidly left him and the broken bones which had partly penetrated his lungs had been eased back into place by Miambo himself, his knowledge of anatomy by no means limited. Bound about with strong linen bandaging, Anjani felt himself again— almost—before the week was out.

To the surprise of Miambo, Anjani appeared in his dwelling a couple of days before the week had expired.

"I leave, Wise One," Anjani said.

"And go where, my son? You are not a fit man."

"I am well enough to move, and I *must* go. Already I may be too late. I have to pick up the trail of the white woman. I shall call Imbazi, the elephant, to carry me."

"So be it then, Anjani," Miambo sighed. "We shall miss you."

"I shall return often, Wise One—and if I can, I shall bring much prosperity and trade to the Untani. If I find gold and ivory in Akada, I shall use only the Untani to remove it."

With that Anjani took his departure, disregarding all provisions since the jungle could feed him. Weapons, too, he ignored. His knife was quite sufficient. He felt better as he crossed the compound in the blazing heat. Nature and the sun could heal more quickly than all the potions and hours of lying on a raffia bed. Lamina watched him go.

Once beyond the stockade, Anjani looked about him, then began to climb the nearest tree to the lowermost branches. It was an effort he found considerable, and certainly all hope of leaping from tree to tree in the former manner was ruled out. Bones had still to knit and lungs to heal. So he cupped his hands and issued a shrill, trumpeting scream. The weird cry penetrated and echoed to the furthest depths of the mighty forest. Animals heard it and knew it for what it was: the cry of the forest white god calling to Imbazi the elephant.

After the fifth call, he relaxed and waited. An hour passed, then just as he was thinking he should send forth another call he caught the distant sounding of smashing undergrowth and rustling of branches. Before very long a monstrous grey shape loomed below, vast ears flapping to keep away the eternal flies.

"Imbazi!" Anjani cried, rising up on the tree branch. "Imbazi! Here!"

The bull elephant, an enormous specimen, trumpeted in welcome and came lumbering forward. Anjani smiled as he watched. This was the same faithful creature who always responded to his call, a battle-scarred old warrior who had formed a mysterious link of animal kinship with the giant white man—possibly on account of the fact that Anjani had once freed the elephant when it had became ensnared in an elephant trap.

Lightly Anjani vaulted down onto the broad back and tapped the colossal cranium with one hand.

"Move," he told the beast, and guided him by a simple dig of his bare heel into the armour-plated skin.

The elephant did as ordered, a living tank that ploughed down the small trees and undergrowth in its path. And as he went, Anjani listened intently to the chattering of the monkeys in the treetops.

In the monkeys, observers of everything that happened around them, he had perfect informers. By gauging their state of agitation, he had indirect evidence of whether or not something out of the ordinary, and threatening—such as human beings—had crossed their path.

By degrees, and with considerable difficulty, Anjani finally came upon a visible trail stretching into the jungle beyond the blackened re-growing area where the fire had been.

Anjani tapped the animal's head round and it lumbered dutifully in a new direction.

So, finally, after three hours of progress—which would have taken a human a good six, with the screen of jungle to smash down—the elephant arrived at the swift-flowing river where the crocodiles spawned. And here the trail completely disappeared. Anjani looked about him, troubled.

For the elephant to cross the river would not have been difficult, but it would never survive the crocodiles. It seemed likely to Anjani that the trail continued on the opposite bank. But how to cross?

Then Anjani remembered as he identified this particular torrent. It continued for a couple of miles, then narrowed abruptly before widening out again into falls. There was just a chance a crossing could be made at the narrowest point.

"Move on, Imbazi," he commanded, kicking his heel, and the elephant turned obediently and ploughed its way along the riverbank, moving with greater speed now since there was less obstruction in the form of vegetation.

Anjani kept an anxious watch on the river, hoping his expectations would prove correct and that he had not confused this torrent with some other, Then, at length, he realised he had been right, for the banks were showing distinct signs of coming closer together and the thunder of falls rose on the shimmering air.

At length the banks were at their closest approach before widening out again to the falls. Anjani edged the elephant gently forward until it stood, trunk upraised, only a few inches from the water's edge.

Keenly Anjani studied the water. It was fast moving here, and for that very reason prevented any activity by crocodiles. How deep it was he did not know. Nor did he know if the faithful elephant could make the trip to the other side—not very far distant—without being swept away. Finally he decided to leave it to the pachyderm's own judgment. Its own instincts would tell it if it had a chance of survival.

"Forward, Imbazi," Anjani murmured in the huge ear, dug his heels, and then waited tensely.

The elephant moved down to the water's edge and put his front feet in it. He trumpeted shrilly, surveyed the opposite bank with short-sighted gaze, and then want on again. The shelf on the bank gave way under the monster's weight and Anjani found himself with water surging round his waist.

But the elephant knew exactly what he was doing and kept on swimming, trunk swinging out of the water, massive legs propelling him broadside to the current. He made the short gap without undue difficulty and lumbered up on the opposite side, trumpeting again in triumph.

"Good, good," Anjani congratulated him, patting the vast neck. "Onward, Imbazi. Anjani seeks the white woman."

Though the elephant did not understand this in the least, it did gather that it was being flattered for its work, so it moved with an extra spirit, smashing down every barrier.

Then Anjani picked up the trail again, and the elephant turned with inexhaustible strength and continued going. Anjani kept up the pace until they reached a jungle stream and clearing. Here he permitted a halt and was lifted down gently from the pachyderm's back. He had a meal of fruits and juice, while the elephant sucked water through its trunk and blew the contents over its back. Then, after a short rest, man and beast were on their way again.

And the trail seemed interminable, even though the elephant was following it nearly six times faster than the humans who had made it. The spurring thought to Anjani was that it looked as if the girl was still alive, even though she was probably in the company of Moon and Tocoto.

Until nightfall Anjani continued on his journey, never once missing the trail, because the monkeys were always there to inform him. Here and there a jungle beast slunk into view to give battle, then withdrew as the foe became revealed as the huge elephant.

With coming of the darkness, the trail was invisible and Anjani made it an opportunity to rest. He started a fire in the clearing, covered himself in vegetable leaves, and relaxed. The elephant, since he had not received a dismissal, made no attempt to stray away and slept too, after his own fashion. Then at dawn, after the usual fruit breakfast, Anjani was on his way again. He stopped at the first stream he came to whilst the elephant drank copiously. As far as food was concerned, he contented himself with herbivorous fodder as he went along.

The further he travelled, the more Anjani realised how completely the three people he was following were off-trail—if it was Akada they were heading for, as he assumed. They were already off the course, and the divergence became greater as time went on. In fact, the party had turned an almost complete circle in the jungle and were heading back in the direction from which they had come. Whether this was intentional or not, Anjani had no idea; he could only spur his gigantic mount to greater endeavours, and being a living battering-ram the animal travelled infinitely faster than any humans had ever done. Anjani did not know it, of course, but it was undoubtedly this circling that had made Tocoto suspicious.

The day passed, and the night again, and another day before Anjani, becoming weary of the chase, came into a clearing where the main trail appeared to end. In the saturating heat of the afternoon he looked about him. There were the dead ashes of a fire, several wilted leaves that looked as though they had done service as beds, and a number of footprint trails going back and forth in the soft earth. Anjani considered the imprints for a while, puzzled, and then murmured to the elephant who promptly lifted him down with his trunk. Quickly Anjani searched the clearing, and it was not long before he came upon two trails leading into the jungle. He followed first one, then the other, on foot, and found that they presently converged into one, extending away into the density of the forest. So even now the journey was not ended.

Returning to the elephant, he was swung up once more to its back, and he urged the great creature to all the speed he could muster. Bushes, vines, screens of vegetation—they all fell before the pounding of the mighty legs and the shoving of the huge head. Mile after mile they crashed through the jungle, and all the time Anjani kept on the alert. He was not aware, so much noise did the elephant make, that he overtook Tocoto swinging through the trees not very far above. Tocoto saw the elephant and Anjani pass below him and stared in amazement—but fast though he began to move, he was not able to keep up with the speeding pachyderm.

It was when the trail became obviously newly made, some of the bent saplings not having yet straightened from being brushed against, that Anjani slowed down. He was very close now—and he expected to see Tocoto, Rita, and the trader. He kept the elephant at a crawl, listening alertly, but the noise of the giant feet was too obliterating. So he slid to the ground, trusting the elephant to wait for him, and then went ahead on foot.

Presently he was glad he had, for he came upon them unexpected, and only had a second's chance to dodge out of sight. In a clearing were Rita and the fat trader, and no sign of Tocoto. Apparently some kind of argument was in progress, the trader gripping Rita's arm fiercely and holding her tightly. She talked too rapidly and angrily for Anjani to gather what she said. But actions were enough. It was plain that the trader was doing his utmost to overpower her and force her to the ground.

Anjani almost dashed out of concealment to deal with the situation, then he hesitated. He was still not by any means in perfect condition, and any hard fighting with the trader might easily incapacitate him again, which would make things worse than ever. Even as he thought on these things, he swung round and raced back to where his giant mount was patiently waiting, tossing his enormous head irritably amidst the flies.

Quickly Anjani clambered onto the elephant's back, digging his heels to spur the animal to go into the clearing ahead. He began moving quickly, his huge body shaking the earth,

Moon had just forced Rita to the ground when the elephant smashed through the foliage, trumpeting shrilly. The trader straightened immediately, staring in alarm. Rita gave a scream, believing she had escaped one fate only to run into another. She lay where she had fallen, petrified to the spot.

This gave Anjani the chance he was waiting for.

As Moon began to run away from Rita, so Anjani dug his heel, prompting the elephant to veer away from Rita and follow in Moon's direction.

Bending low, near to one of the huge flapping ears, Anjani then uttered a weird, piercing scream. It was a passable imitation of an enraged bull elephant—which cry Anjani had heard several times in his jungle career. He repeated the chilling cry.

The effect of his cries on the elephant was exactly as Anjani had calculated, as it hurtled on gigantic feet straight towards the fleeing Moon.

Moon never reached the edge of the clearing. He shrieked in terror as, still trumpeting in fury, the elephant bore down on him, mighty forelegs smashing downwards with a force of several tons. Instantly the trader was crushed into the earth, his gross body becoming a doormat for the restless feet. Nor did the pachyderm finish with this. He finally seized the broken, bleeding thing that had been a man in his trunk, waved him aloft, then flung him with terrific force into the surrounding screen of vegetation. Not that Moon was aware of it. Life had ceased at the instant those huge feet had crushed down on his unprotected head.

Triumphant, still trumpeting, Imbazi swung round. Rita had got to her feet by now and was about to try a run for safety.

Wide-eyed, she waited, convinced that sooner or later the elephant would reveal its fury. She would try and dodge to one side—

She tensed as she heard further strange cries—but these were much lower in tone, almost soothing. The elephant slowed to a halt, a dozen yards from her. Then she gave a gasping cry of thankfulness as a tall white man in a leopard skin suddenly became visible, standing up from the elephant's back.

He leapt nimbly to the ground.

"Anjani!" she cried hoarsely, nearly crying in relief. "Anjani—!"

Half laughing, half laughing, Rita rushed into Anjani's arms. He held her for a long moment, then gently released her and stood back. In the background the now-calmed elephant stood more or less motionless except for his huge ears flapping irritably,

"I found you in time," Anjani said.

"Yes—yes. But—how did you know—? What has been happening? Harry! What has happened to him?"

Anjani was silent. Rita's expression changed a little.

"Then it is true? Caleb Moon told me that Harry was killed by a gorilla...."

"He spoke the truth. I saw it happen. I was nearly killed too. I am still bandaged, as you can see. I came with all speed."

Rita remained silent. Anjani motioned to the cool undergrowth and she seated herself, gazing moodily into the sunlit forest. Not far above her Tocoto was poised, fuming. He had witnessed the slaying of Caleb Moon, and would have liked nothing better at the moment than to plunge down onto this partly incapacitated white rival and destroy him—and the woman, too, unless she might be forced to show him where Akada lay. But Tocoto knew better than to risk the insane jealous fury of the elephant who stood passively by. As he had dealt with Moon, so he would deal with Tocoto—if he dared attack.

Tocoto in fact was very much beaten. He could not even understand the language in which the two were conversing below—but he *did* understand the vision of the map that Anjani presently brought from his loincloth. Rita looked at it for a moment in amazement,

"You—you managed to save it, then?"

Anjani nodded and told her how. He also told her the story which Miambo had told him, which seemed to suggest he was the rightful owner of the map.

"Yes, it's probably true," Rita agreed finally. "Moon

never did say how he got hold of the map. Knowing him, I imagine it would be by some illegal procedure. Maybe he even stole it from some member of the expedition who had been carrying it around with him—not that it matters now, with Moon having been crushed to death by—by your elephant."

"Imbazi." Anjani smiled grimly. "He deserved it— as does Tocoto, who dares to rival me. Some day I shall seek him out and deal with him too."

Tocoto, hearing his own name, pricked up his ears in the foliage above and seethed at his inability to understand.

"I don't think you should blame Tocoto," Rita said, laying a hand on Anjani's powerful arm. "He is a wild creature, even as you are, but he never caused me any uneasiness, and indeed performed many acts of courage. But for him, Moon would probably have defiled or killed me long since."

Anjani shook his blond head. "There cannot be two lords in one jungle, white woman."

Rita looked at the map he hag given her and sighed.

"This all seems so useless now Harry's gone," she muttered. "He was the one who was so desperately anxious to find Akada—not so much to add to the money he already had, and which will now become mine, but to gain the trading rights. He had one ambition: to control—in comfort if he could—nearly all the trading rights for ivory and gold throughout Africa.... But you won't understand that, Anjani."

Anjani smiled as he handed her an opened fruit,

which she accepted gratefully.

"Perhaps I do," he responded. "My tribe, the Untani, do trading too, of sorts. It is not much different from that of the 'civilised' men.... I have a plan," he hesitated. "Rita!"

"That's better, Anjani," she said, laughing.

"My plan, Rita, is that we continue to Akada as before. I know the way without the map, as I told you—but now we have the map, which I give to you, we cannot fail. We are not very far away. Five days, perhaps more."

"But is it worth it?" Rita asked, shrugging. "It might not yield anything when we get there, and as far as money is concerned, I do not need any more. The Perrivale millions are world famous."

"I do not understand millions, Rita, nor their meaning to you. But I do understand trade. If we do find gold and ivory in Akada, you will need many carriers to remove it. My tribe can provide them—on conditions."

"Conditions?" Rita looked surprised. It seemed odd for a man of the jungle, despite his very fair grasp of the English language, to talk of 'conditions.'

"I ask that the Untani become the sole jungle owners of the gold and ivory you get, and that you pay them for their work in moving it."

It was a moment or two before Rita grasped the fundamentals of the proposition, and when she did she gave a half smile.

"You mean you want your tribe to be the exclusive African agents for everything I have removed from

Akada—and they get a percentage of the returns, either in goods or some form which is of value to them?"

Anjani asked for the explanation of one or two words and then he nodded.

"Yes," he assented simply. "Miambo, head of the tribe, as I told you, is a very wise man. He deserves to prosper, and will—with the rest of tribe—if you agree to my plan. I owe them much for rearing me and saving my life."

"But of course I agree!" Rita exclaimed. "The stuff can't be removed without help, and help has to be paid for anywhere in the world. I'd as soon give it to your tribe as anybody." She paused, looking at him steadily. "Which means we go to Akada?"

He nodded.

"At least we can go in peace," she reflected. "I don't think there are any enemies left."

"Only Tocoto," Anjani said.

"True," Rita admitted, "but I've come to the conclusion by now that he's written everything off as a bad job, otherwise he would surely have attacked me, or Moon? Unless he lost the trail, of course. In any case he doesn't signify now you are here. Tocoto cannot stand against you—or at least I hope not. You are still not a fit man, Anjani."

Tocoto withdrew slightly into the foliage as he saw Anjani glance above him.

"You realise," Rita asked presently, resting her head on Anjani's shoulder as they perched on the elephant's back, "that you are as white-skinned as I am?"

"Yes, and for that reason Tocoto might try to take you from me. Not now, but *sometime*. If for no other reason than that, I must kill him."

Rita opened her eyes wider as a thought occurred to her.

"You may not know it, Anjani, but you almost proposed to me!" she exclaimed.

"Proposed?" He looked puzzled.

"Yes. You said Tocoto might try to take me from you, which means you want me. In a more civilised way that would have read—'I'm very much in love with you, and want to marry you.' In other words you would like me for your mate."

Anjani gave a rather gloomy smile. "I would like you for mate, yes," he admitted, "but it is not possible, You and I—me—are of different worlds."

"Not at all—" Rita was fully awake again by now. "Oh, I see what you mean! You live in this jungle and I live in civilisation—so-called. That's easily remedied. You must come back to Port Durnford with me and behave as becomes a normal white man. We might even be able to trace your name and find out what your family is like. You may even be a wealthy man and don't know it."

The elephant lumbered on steadily as Anjani pondered. Then at last he shook his head.

"I not wish for civilisation," he said simply. "Here is my home. I stay."

"But—but it's absurd! You only got here by acci-dent, same as your brother. You can't honestly mean you prefer this wild and savage life when you could have comforts?"

Anjani looked into Rita's wide grey eyes. "Yes, Rita, that is what I mean. Here are my friends—even old Imbazi here—and Miambo. I could not leave them." He shrugged his shoulders. "What is comfort? I do not know."

Rita was silent. She had the feeling that she had fought a tough battle and lost it. After a long period of silence, Anjani looked down on her again.

"You forget mate who died?" he asked, with a touch of dryness.

"Harry? No. I haven't forgotten—but there was a good deal that Harry and I didn't agree about. Losing him doesn't hurt as much as I had thought it would. When I married him—became his mate—I made—a mistake. Now he has gone I naturally want somebody to—well, to help me. I'm not the kind of woman who can live to herself."

"I not leave jungle, Rita, even for you," Anjani decided, and with that the subject seemed to drop. Rita sighed, relaxed again in his arms, and fell asleep. The next thing she knew she was being lifted down gently from the elephant's back and the night had come.

She stood for a moment returning to wakefulness and held by Anjani's powerful arm, then he motioned for her to be seated. As she settled, she looked about her. Evidently Anjani had been busy whilst she had slept. A fire was turning in the clearing centre and over it hung some small animal roasting slowly. In two half-shells of a coconut was juice for drinking. In fact, within jungle limits, Anjani had prepared quite a repast. Even the elephant was busy feeding on the vegetation and occasionally thrusting his trunk into the nearby stream.

"We stay night," Anjani explained, as he settled beside the girl. "Both of us sleep in peace. Imbazi will guard us."

"And how soon do you think we'll reach Akada?" Rita asked.

"Four or five days maybe. That does not trouble me. What *does* trouble me is: where is Tocoto? Is he watching us, is he gathering a tribe to attack us, or what *is* he doing?"

"Following us, I suppose," Rita replied, with a half apprehensive glance to the darkness of the surrounding trees. "He is trying to find Akada because of a jewel it possesses which will give him power over the tribes of the forest."

"I hear of it," Anjani said moodily. "But I not believe a jewel can do that."

"Not of itself, perhaps, but the psychological effect might be pretty powerful."

This comment sailed entirely over Anjani's head and he merely shrugged. And in the trees not far above him Tocoto remained silent, watching and waiting, preparing to doze and move on again in the wake of the two when the dawn came. Even if he could not keep up with them at the speed the elephant travelled, he could certainly follow the trail. That was one thing about Imbazi: he certainly left a track behind him! But Tocoto had to watch that the elephant didn't scent him.

CHAPTER EIGHT
IN THE TREASURE VAULT

When the sun was high the following morning Anjani and Rita, perched as usual on the elephant's back, came suddenly in sight of the cliff shaped like a demon's ear. It lay at a point where the jungle had thinned and instead there lay a shelving valley filled with smaller tropical verdure. At the other side of it, quivering in the heat waves, reared the cliff, reddish in colour, and exactly like the ear of a demon with its pointed apex and steeply curved lobe.

"Yes, that's a simian ear all right," Rita confirmed, as she studied it. "We can't be so far away now, Anjani—and we're getting out of the jungle into open country."

He nodded. In the distance striped hyenas were wandering, hardly distinguishable from the grass.

"We bear north from here," Rita added, studying the map, "and that ought to bring us to a plateau from which we should see a three-peaked mountain range. If we do, it is nearly journey's end, for Akada lies beyond that range."

"Which is as I remember it," Anjani conceded, and he gave the elephant a tap with his heels to start him going again.

It took the great beast, with halts at water holes and streams, until mid-afternoon to cover the approximate fifteen miles along the valley side to where it rose suddenly into a flat plateau. Far away in the distance, nearly hidden by the eternal quivering of the air, loomed the purple of a mountain range, three distinct peaks towering to the tropical sky,

"That's it!! Rita cried excitedly.

Anjani nodded, but did not seem too enthusiastic. Then he explained why.

"Many, many miles," he said. "Open land with no water and few growing things. I remember this part of the country. There are rocks here where few things can grow. We stay here for rest and start tomorrow. Must begin journey feeling refreshed—as must poor old Imbazi too."

He jumped down to the elephant's trunk and was swung to the ground, Rita following him. They looked about them, selected a shady spot in which to rest, and then began the eternal search for fruit. Just here the jungle ended. Henceforth, they would only be able to rely on whatever they could take with them. They considered this prospect when finally they were seated, eating and drinking, allowing the elephant to roam as it wished.

"I very much doubt," Anjani said, with a glance towards the pachyderm. "If Imbazi will carry us any further. Though he loves to obey me, he also obeys his instincts. When he knows there is no water ahead, and no food of the type to suit him, I think he'll become obstinate."

"Which means we go on foot?" Rita asked, gazing out over the semi-volcanic waste.

"There is no other way."

She became silent, making up her mind to herself. Since she had come this far, she might as well finish the job, gruelling though it might prove.

And Anjani's guess proved right. The creature shifted its feet uneasily, surveyed the waste and trumpeted, then turned and went lumbering away into the forest. There was a final view of his absurd little tail and vast rear, then the bushes and trees closed around him. Tocoto saw him go too, and his eyes gleamed. He had just caught up with the two he sought, and now surveyed them from the trees.

In fact, he was on the point of acting, but before he could do so Anjani and the girl started forward in sudden resolve into the scrubby wilderness, carrying with them a number of fruits fastened together with thongs. Tocoto's chance was gone. Now that he no longer had trees to conceal his movements and make a sudden surprise possible, he knew it was more than likely that Anjani, prepared, would be ready to grapple with any attack. Anjani was now back to his former state of health. So Tocoto looked into the distances where lay the mountain range and decided what she should do next. Akada was that way; that much he had gathered. If he arrived there *first*...? He nodded to himself, waited until Anjani and Rita were a considerable way off across the waste, and then he started moving in a wide detour, using folds and hummocks in the ground to conceal his movements.

Meanwhile, entirely unaware that they were being bypassed, Anjani and Rita pressed on. This, definitely, was the hardest part of the journey, seeming even more so after the comparatively comfortable progress they had made on the back of the elephant. The ground was hard and bare and scorching hot; the sun blazed with relentless African force from a cloudless sky. Even Anjani, accustomed to the outdoors and the furious climate, found his spirits flagging somewhat. Rita was uncomplaining, but fast becoming exhausted. Already her vegetation shoes had been cut to pieces by the hard ground with the result that she had to pick her way forward as best she could.

Finally Anjani could stand it no longer. He swept her up into his arms and held her there.

"My feet hard as the rocks," he explained. "I do not feel the stone or the heat. When we reach better ground I will set you down again."

But the 'better ground' he hoped for was not gained until the early evening when the sun was fast sinking, by which time Anjani had come to more or less grassy land and the mountains were considerably nearer. He set down Rita and smiled at her. She tried to smile back but the heat seemed to have sapped the life out of her.

"We rest and refresh," he said, and squatted down.

They spent two hours recovering their strength, by which time the night had come. The air cooled somewhat and enabled them to continue—so, in spells, throughout the night, they continued their journey, and to their relief the dawn found them in the mountain foothills with a gigantic cleft straight ahead of them.

"The gateway to Akada!" Anjani cried in delight, staring at it. "I remember it! City just beyond there!"

Rita, held in the grip of his powerful arm, nodded wearily and they began advancing again. In another half-hour they had reached the pass. Half an hour after that they were at its opposite end, hemmed in by frowning walls. But ahead of them, plainly visible in the glare of the morning, was their goal.

Akada was like something out of the past. It might even have been the mythical El Dorado, which a Spanish sailor had once glimpsed. In fact, it might have been anything—a remnant of a lost and highly artistic civilisation. To the tired man and nearly collapsing girl it was a crumbling city of tall, stately minarets, pagoda-like towers, and one-storey buildings. The once broad streets were cracked now where vegetation had forced its way through. The great terraces and colonnades were almost hidden by creepers, which had dug their relentless tendrils into the cracks and spaces.

Dead—utterly dead.

"Where do you suppose the gold and ivory is hidden?" Rita asked at last, stirring in Anjani's grip.

"I can go to it," Anjani replied. "It is under the ground, in the place of the dead. Have you enough strength to finish the journey?"

Rita shook her head. "I must rest, Anjani. I'm all in."

He nodded and laid her down amidst the warm undergrowth in the rocks. Removing the thronged fruits from his shoulder, he prepared one for her, but by the time he had handed it down she was fast asleep. He smiled gravely and settled down beside her, prepared to wait until she had recovered.

Nature took her time. Rita slept all day, protected by the vegetable leaves Anjani spread over here as the sun climbed higher. Then, towards evening, she showed signs of stirring. Refreshed again she looked at him with brighter eyes.

"Here," he said, handing her some fruit. "You have slept long. You feel better?"

"Much. I'm not like you, remember—cast iron."

"Just the same, you very strong," Anjani responded. "Few women could have done as much."

He did his best to conceal the fact that he was impatient to be on his way, but he need not have worried, for the moment Rita had finished drinking the juice and eating the fruit, she scrambled to her feet. She stretched her arms, then looked at Akada.

"I'm ready if you are," she said, over her shoulder.

Immediately Anjani joined her and, his hand about her waist to support her, he walked with her down the rubble-strewn slope that led to what had once been the main square of the town. Since the sun was rapidly setting, Anjani increased his pace and Rita submitted to being led in and out of the grassy terraces, between the huge and weather-eroded colonnades, and so at last to a half-obliterated oblong opening in the ground to which there led worn stone steps.

"Just as I last saw it," Anjani murmured. "The great stone which covers the opening is tilted to one side—as you see—and below is the gold and ivory. How it got there I do not know. Perhaps it belonged to the people of this race; perhaps other men put it there and could never find Akada afterwards. See—I will show you."

Turning aside, he selected a dry branch, then collected a little heap of bone-dry dust and a thin stick. In a matter of a few minutes he had kindled a small fire, from which he lighted the branch for use as an improvised torch. When it was flaming brightly he led the way down the steps, past the huge stone that normally closed up the opening, and then into a cavernous blackness. Rita hung onto his arm, awed by her entry into this long lost storehouse,

Anjani penetrated perhaps a quarter of a mile through the torch-flickered darkness before he stopped. Rita held onto him, her eyes wide in amazement.

"There!" Anjani whispered. "Was I not right?"

"But—this is unbelievable!" Rita cried. "The value of all this stuff! Why, it's—"

Words failed her. She was looking on treasure of stupendous value. All one wall was stacked to the ceiling with yellow ivory, and against the opposite wall were gold ingots, reflecting a dull saffron glow from the torchlight. To Rita there could only be one answer: this was not the hoard of a tropical expedition. It must have belonged to the vanished race that had built Akada. The gold alone was worth millions.

"There for the taking," she said at last.

"The Untani can move it for you," Anjani answered. "They can either move it to the east or west, as you wish."

"It would be quickest to have it transported to Loango in Equatorial Africa," Rita mused. "We are much nearer to that coast than the other."

At the entrance to the underground treasure Tocoto stood listening and smiling bitterly to himself. After a while he opened his tightly clenched left hand and studied the liquid fire glowing in his palm. A ruby of extraordinary size and lustre lay there, a ruby which he had removed from the main temple of the deserted city. He had accomplished his purpose as much as Anjani and Rita had accomplished theirs.

The voices came clearly to Tocoto along the narrow tunnel, but as on other occasions he could not understand the language. Finally he turned away and studied the immense stone, which had been drawn aside from the tunnel opening by the earlier expedition, with which Anjani—as a boy—had travelled.

The first sign of Tocoto's activities came to Anjani and Rita when, as they studied the ivory in the wavering light of the expiring torch, they heard a heavy crash— an earthy, reverberating thud, at the end of the tunnel. A cloud of dust came sweeping in towards them and the walls of the underground place quivered for a moment.

"That—that sounds like a stone falling over the entrance way!" Rita exclaimed in alarm.

Anjani's face was grim in the nearly vanished torchlight. He swung round and raced back up the tunnel, to meet a solid blackness where formerly there had been an opening. In a second or two Rita had caught up with him.

"This is Tocoto," Anjani muttered, staring at the barrier. "That stone could never have fallen itself. It must have been pushed."

He broke off as a voice using tribal jargon reached whim from outside.

"Can you hear me, Anjani? White woman?"

"I hear," Anjani shouted back, and Rita waited anxiously to receive an interpretation.

"You and the white woman sought the treasures of Akada—and found them! Now you can die with them! You know the law of the jungle, Anjani! There cannot be two masters. If I do not destroy you, you will destroy me. I have been clever. I have trapped you. We shall never meet in physical combat.... And in my hand I have power! Power over all the tribes of the jungle. The jewel of Akada! I can make every tribe every-where obey my bidding. Tocoto's name shall be known and feared from one end of the jungle to the other...."

The voice died away and there was a heavy silence. The last glimmer went from the torch and pitch darkness descended.

"Who was that?" Rita demanded, clutching Anjani's arm. "Was it Tocoto?"

"It was." Anjani's voice was grim. Then he went on to interpret what he had said.

"And do you think that jewel he has stolen *will* give

him the power he speaks of?"

"It may. The natives are but children—you yourself said not very long ago that it would have an effect."

"A psychological effect, yes. I remember saying that. It means Tocoto can become lord of the jungle by reason of a mystical power—real or imaginary—which he now possesses. But what can we do? Is there no way out of this ghastly place?"

"We must find one," Anjani answered, but though he sounded purposeful, there was a dubious note in his voice.

He began moving in the darkness, Rita still hanging on to his arms in case she became separated. For about the first time in her experiences she was genuinely frightened. The darkness was crushing, and the silence—save for the sounds she and Anjani made—absolute.

Gradually they made their way round the walls, investigating them carefully with their finger ends, tapping the floor with their feet in the hope of finding crevices, which might be widened and give access to a tunnel below—but they found nothing interesting. In the end they came back to the barrier.

"There's got to be some way!" Rita exclaimed desperately. "We can't just rot here after all we've been through."

Anjani did not answer. He was feeling the vast stone that had been rolled over the opening. Rita could not see him but she could hear his movements and the sound of his hard breathing as he strained his powerful muscles.

"Tocoto simply pushed this stone off balance," he said at length. "So naturally it dropped right across the opening. I am wondering if I have strength enough to push it aside, only slightly."

Again came the sound of him straining and breathing. Rita found the barrier and edged her own relatively useless strength against it. When Anjani spoke again, he sounded a little more hopeful.

"My feet keep slipping on the floor. Quickly—we can lay the yellow bricks along the floor to the opposite wall, end to end, and they will make something for me to push against with my feet."

Again the hurried movements in the darkness, the feeling around for the gold stored against the wall. It could half an hour to arrange the yellow metal in a V-shaped carpet to suit Anjani's purpose. Then he placed his massive back to the stone barrier and wedged his heels against the nearest ingot. This time he did not slip since, in effect, the opposite wall was his brace. But he had to desist almost immediately as the metal cut into his feet. Immediately Rita tugged away her vegetable garments in the darkness and laid them against the ingots.

"That's better." Anjani murmured, and began to push with every vestige of his giant strength. He kept it up without a pause for perhaps fifteen seconds and then, to his delight, he felt the huge block move ever so slightly outwards.

Panting, perspiration trickling down his great body,

he relaxed again.

"I think we stand a chance," he said, after a moment. "Get an ivory tusk and use it under the stone. As I push, wedge the tusk. That will stop the stone falling back again."

"Right," Rita agreed promptly, and felt her way through the eye-aching darkness until she came to the stacked piles of ivory. She felt for the nearest tusk but found it quite impossible to lift it. She called to Anjani and told him. Immediately Anjani came to her aid, hauled the tusk from amongst its fellows, and dragged it to the position he wanted. The tip of it he inserted under the edge of the stone block, using his fingers to guide him, then the heavy end he laid carefully over Rita's shoulder. She staggered a little then braced her legs and held firm.

"You can hold that?" he asked her.

"Yes—yes, I'll try. If I've a dent in my shoulder when we get out, I'll know why. I never thought tusks could be so heavy."

Anjani put his back to the stone once more, and heaved with all his power. As fast as he did so, Rita worked the tusk as quickly as she could, and a few more inches were gained.... A pause, then the same thing again—and this time a thin grey line came into view, set with stars.

"The outside!" Rita whooped. "Look! The night sky."

Anjani, stirred to fresh activity by this heartening sight, wedged his fingers in the narrow crack. He preferred this method since it did not inflict such a strain on his still not perfectly healed lungs. He paused for a moment and then threw himself into a tremendous, straining effort.

Rita was so astonished at the stupendous strength of the jungle man she nearly forgot to assist with the task. She saw the gap widening very slowly as, using all the power of his great muscles and the other side of the wall to brace himself, Anjani forced the gap wider, and wider still. At last he stopped, panting for breath, with a two-foot gap clearly visible.

"Come," he said, grasping the girl's arm. "We can get out now."

He squeezed himself through the narrow gap and helped Rita after him. They straightened up thankfully in the cool wind of the night, the tall grass waving gently around them.

"Thank heaven," Rita whispered, drawing her scanty remains of garments about her. "We got free—"

"And Tocoto escapes," Anjani muttered, clenching his fists in the starlight. "I can never catch him...at the moment."

"Why not? You can reach the jungle, call the elephant to help you, and—"

"I have you to look after," he interrupted.

"Oh! I—I forgot. I am a terrific hindrance, I suppose."

There was silence. Anjani's sole desire in life at that moment was to start off in pursuit of his twin and rival, but his sense of duty held him back. He knew the girl could not probably survive without him.

"Later," he muttered. "A day will come when my path and Tocoto's will cross—a day when you will be in safety and I can fight freely. A day when my body will be completely healed. Meanwhile, we must return."

"Return, to where?" Rita asked.

"The Untani, my tribe. You will wish them to remove these treasures, do you not?"

"Certainly, but I'm leaving that to you. I have to make arrangements for the stuff to be shipped. I cannot discuss the matter with your tribe: that is your task. My main object now is to get to Loango on the west coast. From there I can make the necessary shipping contacts...." Rita was silent for a moment, then she added simply, "I know it delays your return to the Untani, but I just can't reach Loango alone. I've no sense of direction."

"We go together," Anjani said gently, his great arm moving protectively about her shoulder. "I not know Loango, but I can reach the west coast. Then we can find our way—"

"A thought occurs to me," Rita interrupted. "Suppose, while we were away, Tocoto makes arrangements to take away this stuff?"

Anjani shook his head. "He only wants the jewel of Akada—and he has it. He does not know the value of ivory and gold. In the jungle such things have no value, except through a trader, as you are. No, he will not come back here. He will believe me dead—and you—and will try and become the unquestioned lord of the jungle. But that can never be whilst I live. Now come. We can begin our journey westwards."

"Can you close up the opening first, just in case Tocoto should be inclined to come back? He'll probably think we're still sealed up behind the stone."

Anjani nodded, put his back against the stone, and shoved with all his huge strength. This time the task was not so difficult. Since the stone was downwardly tilted it dropped back into place easily, completely sealing the gap. This done, Anjani grasped Rita's arm and led her to the top of the grassy slope. Then they began to move towards the city itself in the starlight, crossing its silent expanse and emerging at the far side, constantly moving westwards.

By the middle of the night they had crossed the valley in which the city lay, and were heading towards the continuation of the pass where it split the mountains in twain. Beyond would be more jungle country.

"I suppose," Rita remarked, as she plodded along beside the silent Anjani, "that nothing will make you change your mind about becoming civilised?"

"I cannot do that—yet. I have the Untani to contact and many things to arrange, in readiness for when you decide to move the treasure."

"I know, but *after* that? What when it's all over? Do you still want to roam about this terrible jungle with nothing more exciting on your mind than perhaps trying to kill your brother? You are cut out for better things than that."

"I only leave jungle when Tocoto destroyed," Anjani

replied stubbornly, and from the silence he maintained thereafter that seemed to be his final answer to the question.

Rita did not pursue the topic any further, but she did make up her mind that, no matter what happened, she would she would never lose touch with Anjani. Both in the sense of being a husband worthy of consideration, and because of his knowledge of the jungle, he was entirely desirable. The one flaw in the whole matter was Tocoto and the power he had now acquired.

They had come beyond the mountain pass, and had the starlit expanse of the jungle country ahead of them before Anjani spoke again.

"The sun will not come yet," he said. "We rest and refresh. And you, perhaps, will wish to fashion new clothes."

Rita glanced down at herself. "I think you're right," she agreed dryly—so they stopped at the first clearing they came to, and she fashioned new garments whilst Anjani lighted a fire. For a while after that, to Rita's alarm, he vanished into the jungle, but she need not have worried. When he returned he was carrying a small animal he had slain for the purposes of food.

So they ate, and drank, and then slept, starting on their journey again towards the dawn. Their way travelled constantly westwards, but after two weeks of journeying had gone by, they were still in the midst of the jungle. Rita began to have doubts as to Anjani's sense of direction.

"I'm sure there's a quicker way to reach the coast!"

she told him, as they pushed on through the vegetation in the scorching morning.

"Yes—but I do not take it," was Anjani's bland response. "I am taking the longer way. Maybe it is the last time I am with you. When I fight Tocoto, I may lose the battle. These days are happy; with Tocoto it will not be."

Rita smiled a little. "I see. So that's it! Well, I can't say that I object. But in spite of everything, I am a little tired of being torn to pieces by thorns and blistered by the sun. When *do* we begin to near our journey's end?"

"Another week maybe."

Anjani continued going. And his judgment of another week's travel was not very far out. Rita, counting the days by the sunrises and sunsets, found that seven had gone by before the jungle country was at last left behind, and they were beginning to near signs of outpost civilisation. And at last there came an hour when their wanderings brought them within seeing distance of the Atlantic rollers and the white outlines of dwellings.

Here Anjani came to a stop, looking wistfully towards the west.

"I go no further," he said. "You safe here. You will find white men ahead where you can get food, clothing, and other things."

"Yes, yes, I know, but—surely you will come with me?"

"No." Anjani shook his head. "If I appear with you, I shall be perhaps forced to become civilised, and I not wish to do so. This is where our paths end, Rita."

She looked down at herself in her weird vegetation dress and shoes, then back to him. He studied her, a grave smile on his handsome, bronzed face.

"How do I get in touch with you when I return?" she asked quietly. "And I *shall* return the moment I've made arrangements to get the ivory and gold shipped. To do it I may have to return to England for a while, but I shall certainly come back. How am I ever to find you?"

Anjani looked about him on the desert and rock into which they had come, then he indicated a distant crag standing by itself and jutting out two arms in the shape of a 'Y'.

"That will be our meeting place," he said. "When you have left me, I shall return with all speed to fight Tocoto, and if possible kill him. When I have done that and brought the Untani to Akada, you will have finished what you wish to do. Return to that rock and wait. You will bring others with you. To help you. Stay until I come, unless I am there first. And I *will* come, Rita, even after many days."

"And if you do not? If Tocoto kills you, what then?"

"Tocoto will not kill me; I shall kill him. But, if anything else happens—if I should fall before a jungle beast—then make your own plans after so much time has elapsed that you think you should. Go on to Akada—"

"How? When I do not know the way?"

Anjani pondered, then made up his mind. "There is

only one answer, Rita. I shall be waiting for you and nothing will stop me. That I promise you."

She nodded slowly. "I shall rely on that," she said, with a quiet smile. Anjani looked at her for a moment, her face sunburned, her grey eyes ranging over his face, blonde hair unkempt and blowing in the hot wind.

"Until we meet, then," he said, and stooped to kiss her.

She hung for a moment in his powerful arms, then he released her and turned his back, striding away actively across the sandy waste. He did not once turn round. For him, it appeared, the chapter was closed.

Rita watched him until the dancing heat waves hid him from sight, then she turned her gaze towards the white outposts, which marked civilisation.

When she glanced back over her shoulder some ten minutes later, there was only the desert and, far beyond it, the towering mystery of the jungle.

Rita turned and, smiling wistfully to herself, continued on her way....

ABOUT THE AUTHOR

British writer JOHN RUSSELL FEARN was born near Manchester, England, in 1908. As a child he devoured the science fiction of Wells and Verne, and was a voracious reader of the Boys' Story Papers. He was also fascinated by the cinema, and first broke into print in 1931 with a series of articles in *Film Weekly*.

He then quickly sold his first novel, *The Intelligence Gigantic*, to the American magazine, *Amazing Stories*. Over the next fifteen years, writing under several pseudonyms, Fearn became one of the most prolific contributors to all of the leading US science fiction pulps, including such legendary publications as *Astounding Stories*, *Startling Stories*, *Thrilling Wonder Stories*, and *Weird Tales*.

During the late 1940s he diversified into writing novels for the UK market, and also created his famous superwoman character, The Golden Amazon, for the prestigious Canadian magazine, the Toronto *Star Weekly*. In the early 1950s in the UK, his fifty-two novels as "Vargo Statten" were bestsellers, most notably his novelization of the film, *Creature from the Black Lagoon*.

Apart from science fiction, he had equal success with westerns, romances, and detective fiction, writing an amazing total of 180 novels—most of them in a period of just ten years—before his early death in 1960. His work has been translated into nine languages, and continues to be reprinted and read worldwide.